More Acclaim for *Bone*

"*Bone* achieves a merciless and deeply moving emotional peak. Fae Myenne Ng has created a remarkable work."
—*Philadelphia Inquirer*

"Ng raises the stakes for Asian-American literature and makes a bid for the arrival of a major American voice. . . . *Bone* is a pioneer work." —*San Francisco Bay Guardian*

"Ng has fashioned a spare, elegant book embedded with small fireworks of imagery and insight."
—*Washington Post Book World*

"Fae Myenne Ng tells her story with astonishing grace."
—John Leonard, National Public Radio

"A masterful debut." —*Women's Review of Books*

"Gritty and moving." —*Los Angeles Times*

"Brutal and poignant, dreamy and gritty, specific to its place and resonant in its implications about what it means to be an American." —*Seattle Times/Post Intelligencer*

"Moving and impressive." —*San Francisco Chronicle*

"Sometimes the best, most artful stories are those told in the simplest language. Such is the case with *Bone*. . .a novel as spare, clean, and lovely as its title." —*Orlando Sentinel*

"With the buoyant parting image, Ng invites comparison to F. Scott Fitzgerald and the last line of *The Great Gatsby*. . . . She invites comparison and, in *Bone*, stands up to it."
—*Trenton Times*

"This is the inside view of Chinatown, one never presented before so eloquently. Fae Myenne Ng is a writer with no pretensions and enormous talent. . . . A whole teeming world comes alive under her pen." —Edmund White

"Fae Myenne Ng's first novel *Bone* is a result of many years of hard work and experience. It is tough and real. *Bone* marks the debut of a writer whose literary skills are fantastic."

—Ishmael Reed

"An instant classic. . . . *Bone* is a stunning first novel, a work of great wisdom and compassion. It is simple in the way that Mozart's music is simple: entire lifetimes of living, suffering, and loving have gone into the crafting of everyday words into profound, artless-seeming art. . . . Fae Myenne Ng is an amazing writer."

—Sau-ling C. Wong, Associate Professor of Asian-American Studies, University of California/ Berkeley, and author of a forthcoming study of Asian-American literature

"Fae Myenne Ng is tough and smart, unflinching in her portrait of two generations, Chinese and Chinese-American, who don't have an easy time with each other. There's a sense of history that can't be escaped by will or wit or wish. I learned a lot from *Bone* about the high cost of living in two worlds—but first I enjoyed the freshness of its voice, its rare combination of humor and unvarnished reality. Fae Myenne Ng is on her way."   —Rosellen Brown

"This is a most impressive first book. In its backward-circling drift through time and memory, it also moves through the quarrels, griefs, hopes and loves of several characters—who are not types or policy statements, but wonderfully alive and particular people—and finally takes the reader far enough out to sea to remind him of his own depths. There is not much more you can ask of a novel, and it happens so rarely it makes me want to applaud when I see it achieved."

—Joel Agee

"*Bone* is a wonderfully strong and honest book. This story of three sisters brought up in San Francisco's Chinatown is beautifully conceived, full of feeling and the sound of the streets. Fae Myenne Ng's writing is sensitive and truthful and there is no doubt that a new voice has come into American letters."   —Frank MacShane

"*Bone* has a pure emotional power; it is fused through with life, its people so real, so human I found myself in tears as I read. The spare style, the moving, backward moving structure of the story work to do what good writing should do: they bring to life in the truest way the very heart of this family, in a narrative that enfolds you as you read, and makes you want to keep reading, and when you finish, to start and read it over again."   —Hannah Green

BONE

BONE

FAE MYENNE NG

HarperPerennial
A Division of HarperCollins*Publishers*

I THANK the magazines and anthologies where portions of this book, in slightly different form, first appeared: *The American Voice, Bostonia Magazine, Harper's Magazine, Home to Stay, The One You Call Sister, The Pushcart Prize XII.*

Bone is a work of fiction. Names, characters, places, and incidents either are the products of the author's imagination or are used fictitiously. Any resemblance to events or persons, living or dead, is entirely coincidental.

A hardcover edition of this book was originally published in 1993 by Hyperion. It is reprinted by arrangement with Hyperion.

HarperCollins books may be purchased for educational, business, or sales promotional use. For information please write: Special Markets Department, HarperCollins Publishers, Inc., 10 East 53rd Street, New York, NY 10022.

First HarperPerennial edition published 1994.

Designed by Margaret M. Wagner

Library of Congress Cataloging-in-Publication Data

Ng, Fae Myenne, 1956–
    Bone / Fae Myenne Ng. — 1st ed.
      p.   cm.
    ISBN 0-06-097592-X
     1. Chinese Americans—California—San Francisco—History—Fiction.
    2. Chinese American families—California—San Francisco—Fiction.
    3. San Francisco (Calif.)—History—Fiction. I. Title.
    PS3564.G25B6   1994
    813'.54—dc20   93-37200

02 03 04 05 RRD H 30 29 28 27 26 25 24 23 22 21

For Ah-Sam

For encouragement,
I thank Eric Ashworth and Pat Mulcahy;
for the long heart, Moira Dryer;
for courage, Mark Coovelis.

FOR generous support during the writing of this book, I thank the Mary Ingraham Bunting Institute of Radcliffe College, the Djerassi Foundation, the D. H. Lawrence Fellowship at the University of New Mexico, Massachusetts Artists Foundation, the MacDowell Colony, National Endowment for the Arts, Writers Exchange Program of Poets & Writers, The San Francisco Foundation's Joseph Henry Jackson Award, Virginia Center for the Creative Arts, and the Corporation of Yaddo.

B O N E

ONE

WE WERE a family of three girls. By Chinese standards, that wasn't lucky. In Chinatown, everyone knew our story. Outsiders jerked their chins, looked at us, shook their heads. We heard things.

"A failed family. That Dulcie Fu. And you know which one: bald Leon. Nothing but daughters."

Leon told us not to care about what people said. "People talking. People jealous." He waved a hand in the air. "Five sons don't make one good daughter."

I'm Leila, the oldest, Mah's first, from before Leon. Ona came next and then Nina. First, Middle, and End Girl. Our order of birth marked us and came to tell more than our given names.

Here's another bone for the gossipmongers. On vacation recently, visiting Nina in New York, I got married. I didn't marry on a whim—don't worry, I didn't do a green-card number. Mason Louie was no stranger. We'd been together four, five years, and it was time.

Leon was the first person I wanted to tell, so I went looking for him in Chinatown. He's not my real father, but he's the one who's been there for me. Like he always told me, it's time that makes a family, not just blood.

Mah and Leon are still married, but after Ona jumped off the Nam, Leon moved out. It was a bad time. Too much happened on Salmon Alley. We don't talk about it. Even the sewing ladies leave it alone. Anyway, it works out better that Mah and Leon don't live in the same place.

When they're not feuding about the past, Leon visits Mah, helps her with the Baby Store, so they see enough of each other.

Leon's got a room at that old-man hotel on Clay Street, the San Fran. There's a toilet and bath on each floor and the lobby's used as a common room. No kitchen. I gave Leon a hot plate but he likes to have his meals either down the block at Uncle's Cafe or over at the Universal Cafe.

Leon's got the same room he had when he was a bachelor going out to sea every forty days. Our Grandpa Leong lived his last days at the San Fran, so it's an important place for us. In this country, the San Fran is our family's oldest place, our beginning place, our new China. The way I see it, Leon's life's kind of made a circle.

In the mornings, Leon likes to sit in the lobby timing the No. 55 Sacramento buses; he likes to hassle the drivers if they're not on time. They humor him, call him Big Boss. It was just after eight when I got to the San Fran, but the lobby was empty. There was a thin comb of morning light on the dusty rose-colored sofa, and the straight-back chairs were still pushed up against the wall, at their tidy night angles. When I pulled the accordion doors of the elevator back, they unfolded into a diamond pattern with a loud clang. I yanked the lever back and held it there until the number 8 floated by on the wheel contraption Leon called the odometer; then I jerked the handle forward and the elevator stopped level to the ninth floor. Leon's room was at the end of the corridor, next to the fire escape.

"Leon?" I knocked. "Leon!" I jiggled the doorknob and it turned. Leon forgets the simplest things—like locking the door: another reason it's better he doesn't live with Mah.

Without Leon, the room looked dingier. There was an old-man smell, and junk all over. Leon was a junk inventor. Very weird stuff. An electric sink. Cookie-tin clocks. Clock lamps. An intercom hooked up to a cash register hooked up to the alarm system. When they lived together, Mah put up with it all: his screws, his odd beginnings of projects scattered all over her kitchen table, on their bedside. But the day after he shipped out on a voyage, she threw everything into the garbage. She called it his *lop sop*. But that didn't stop Leon, who continued inventing on the long voyages. On the ships, his bunk was his only space, so every invention was compact. Leon made a miniature of everything: fan, radio, rice cooker. And he brought them all home.

Leon was a collector, too. Stacks of takeout containers, a pile of aluminum tins. Plastic bags filled with packs of ketchup and sugar. White cans with red letters, government-issue vegetables: sliced beets, waxy green beans, squash. His nightstand was a red restaurant stool cluttered with towers of Styrofoam cups, stacks of restaurant napkins, and a cup of assorted fast-food straws. Metal hangers dangled from the closet doorknob. On the windowsill were bunches of lotus leaves and coils of dried noodles. There were several tin cans: one held balls of knotted red string, another brimmed with tangles of rubber bands. The third was ashy with incense punks. Beyond these tins, I could see Coit Tower.

When I visited Leon, he'd make me coffee, boiling water in a pan and straining the grounds like an herbal tea, and then he'd show me every project he had in progress: alarm clocks, radios, lamps, and tape recorders. He'd read to me from his newspaper piles: *The Chinese Times, The China Daily*

News, Wah Kue, World News, Ming Bao. Leon snipped and saved the best stories for his private collection: Lost Husbands, Runaway Wives, Ungrateful Children.

Leon kept his private stash of money, what he called his Going-Back-to-China fund, in a brown bag tucked into an old blanket of Ona's. I called it his petty-cash bag. I slipped a red envelope inside. It was money from Mah, but Leon wasn't supposed to know. This was their crazy game, and I didn't like being in the middle of it. I also didn't like wandering around Chinatown looking for him, but that's what I had to do, so I clicked the button and shut the door behind me.

When I got downstairs, the lobby was as full and as noisy as the Greyhound bus station. A group of coatless men stood in front of the sofa, barking questions at an old man who was seated there. He'd gotten lost.

"How come you go there?"

"How long?"

"You're home now, savvy?"

"How about we call your daughter?"

The lost man patted his knees and kept his eyes downcast. "Don't know," he muttered in a low voice that hardly seemed a breath. "Don't know. Don't remember. Don't know."

"Move aside!" Manager Lee came rushing out of his office, yelling at someone to pour a cup of boiled water from the thermos for the old man.

The questions started again.

"Why you wander off like that?"

"How many more times you be lucky?"

Manager Lee waved the others away. "Let him drink. Shut up. Go do your day."

I followed Manager Lee into his office and watched him flip through a notebook. He dialed quickly, jabbing his long yellowed nail into the circles. The phone clacked and rattled. Then he looked up at me and said in a harsh tone, "What?!"

I stepped back, a little scared.

"Whatsamattah?" he barked again, this time letting his mouth hang open. "Leon lost, too?"

I said, "He's not in his room."

Manager Lee turned his head and shouted into the phone, "Hello-hello? This, Lee at the San Fran hotel. Can you ask Choi Wei-ling to come to the phone?" He covered the mouthpiece and said to me, "Try the Square."

I nodded my thanks and turned to go. The old guys were putting on their coats and shuffling toward the door. The lost man watched, picking at a hole in the arm of the sofa. Behind him, the gray shapes on the linoleum wall looked like shadows of faces. I didn't want to see Leon end up like that, all alone and lost.

I hated looking for Leon at the Square, seeing him hanging around with those time wasters, so I went and checked a couple of other places first. Uncle's Cafe was just down the corner from the hotel; often Leon passed his mornings there, drinking coffee and reading the newspaper. At Uncle's Cafe, every single table is an old-man table. Old men telling jokes and laughing, but no old Leon. The register lady shook her head at me. No Leon, she said. So I continued, turning onto Waverly Place, the two-block alley famous in the old days as barbers' row. Leon still calls it Fifteen-Cent Alley, after the old-time price of a haircut. Now Waverly Place has everything: there's the First Chinese Baptist Church, the Jeng Sen Buddhism Taoism Asso-

ciation, the Bing-Kong Tong Free Masons, the Four Seas
Restaurant and the Pot Sticker, several travel agencies and
beauty salons, but only one barber shop.

On Washington, I looked into the Shing Kee Grocery,
where Leon sometimes helped sort vegetables, but no luck.
No Leon. I walked down the steps to Woey Loy Goey and
looked for Leon's friend, the head cook. Mr. Wong sat
behind the counter, drinking coffee and reading the newspaper. He glanced up when he saw me and muttered, "The
Square," and then went back to his paper.

I couldn't avoid going there.

THE OVERPASS from the Holiday Inn to Portsmouth Square cast a broad shadow over the playground.
Avoiding the beggars' corner, where the pissy stench was
strongest, I followed the sliver of sunlight along the east
side, crowded with grandmothers and young children.

A group of old men stood at the base of the stairs,
playing cards. The one holding his cards close had a thumb
like a snake's head; he stared at me, so I gave him a scowl.
When I walked past the chess tables, more old guys turned,
more stares. I never liked being the only girl on the upper
level of the park. More than once, an old guy has come up
and asked, "My room? Date?" It was just pathetic.

I heard a raucous laugh, a jeering curse, and then I
recognized You Thin Toy's phlegmy voice. "I eat your
horse!"

The men clustered close together at each table. They
looked like scraps of dark remnant fabric. As I moved
closer, the details became more distinct: tattered collars,
missing buttons, safety-pinned seams, patch pockets full of
fists.

You Thin Toy was buried four men deep, so I pushed into the crowd. He was my personal favorite of Leon's fleabag friends. They met on the S.S. *Lincoln*, coming over to America. Leon was fifteen, You Thin, eighteen, but their false papers gave them each a few extra years. On the long voyage, they coached each other on their paper histories: Leon was the fourth son of a farm worker in the Sacramento valley, his mother had bound feet, her family was from Hoiping. You Thin was the second son of a shoe cobbler in San Francisco, the family compound had ten rooms, the livestock consisted of an ox, two pigs, and many chickens. His older brother was a fishery worker in Monterey and his younger brother worked in San Francisco with their father.

After You Thin and Leon both passed the interrogation at Angel Island, they slapped each other's backs. Each called the other "Brother" and predicted the good life, *"Hao sai gai!"* Leon asked one of the friendlier guards on the Island for a word to describe their blood brotherness.

"Cousin," the guard said.

Maybe "cousin" was Leon's first English word.

You Thin changed back to his real name as soon as he could, but Leon never did. Leon liked to repeat what he told You Thin: "In this country, paper is more precious than blood."

"Pow!" A man slapped down a disk with the character "field." The painted green strokes were brilliant against the concrete table.

"Pow!" the man said again, "my elephant eats your fat queen."

"Wey!" You Thin held on to the back of his head as if it hurt. "Again!" He chanted the names as he reset the chessboard: "Cannon. Elephant. Field."

"Cousin." I tapped his shoulder. "You seen Leon?"

You Thin glanced up and muttered, "The Universal."

As I turned to go, old raspy voices followed me.

"Who's that?"

"Leon's oldest."

"Not bad."

THE UNIVERSAL is my favorite cafe, but not for the food. I like the old-style booths, the marble-topped tables with the bare bulbs overhead, and the soda fountain with the cushioned red stools.

The waiters were filling sugar and napkin containers, getting ready for the Greyhound tour crowds. Fat Croney Kam sat behind the caged register booth. His round head filled the window and he looked like a big plucked bird. Croney Kam pointed with his smooth chin toward the kitchen and said, "Leon's helping out. My no-good fry cook quit. Sell his mother!"

I saw Leon through the horizontal service window. His long neck and bald head reminded me of a light bulb.

I pushed through the swinging doors into the kitchen. "You working all day?"

He smiled. "Just lunch rush. New York fun?"

"Lots."

Croney yelled through the service window, "Three fry wonton!" He winked at me, "Big Miss have time? Give a hand, help Uncle Kam out."

I had time, so I washed my hands and started folding wontons. Leon asked me New York questions.

"You go see Time Square?"

I made a face.

"Brooklyn?"

I shook my head.

"I took the subway be the wrong direction. I saw." From the raised subway tracks, he saw dilapidated buildings and huge cracks in the street. Leon was impressed; he said it was a good name, the right name: Brooklyn was broke.

"What about the Freedom Goddess?"

I had no idea what he was talking about.

"You know." He raised his arm over his head. "Green Lady in Ocean."

I laughed. "Statue of Liberty, Leon."

"What about Chinatown, you go there?"

"Sure, with Nina. Hey, Leon, guess what about Nina."

I saw Leon's worried brow and lowered my voice. "Don't tell Mah but she likes this Chinese guy." I paused. "Chinese from China," I said.

Leon scooped up some wonton and gave the ladle a whack on the rim of the wok. "What happened to that Michael?"

"She's better off without him."

Leon looked surprised and then he pushed a plate toward me on the counter. "Try," he said.

I nibbled on the hot tail of the wonton knot. "Better not tell Mah yet," I warned. "You never know with Nina."

"Don't have to worry. I keep a secret good."

Hearing that made the telling easy. "Guess what else, Leon."

He looked up.

I said, "Mason and me, we got married. In New York."

Leon was quiet for a while and then his straggly brow twitched. "City Hall?"

"Yeah . . . But how'd you know?"

He winked at me, smiling big. "I been there, too."

It took me a minute to catch up with him. I relaxed, remembering that Leon didn't like fanfare and ceremony. He'd already said no flowers, no bugle and drums at his funeral. In matters of the heart, Leon preferred the simple.

What wasn't simple was my guilt about having a better life than Mah. She married my father for a thrill and Leon for convenience. She loves Mason and she'd be happy for us, but she'd have to face her bitterness about her own marriages and that's what I wanted to protect her from. Remembering the bad. Refeeling the mistakes.

"*Wey!* Croney Kam!" Leon was yelling out the service window. "Come congratulate me. My Lei just married the Louie boy."

For a fat man, Croney Kam moved fast. He came belly first through the double doors. "Who?" he demanded, looking at me and then at Leon. "What?"

Leon tapped his chest. "My Lei married the Louie boy."

"Louie? Louie who?"

"You know, Lam-kok Louie, the old herbalist."

"The one who cured old Jue?"

"Yeah. Him. Him grandson."

"Long-hair, that boy?"

"Say something good, why don't you?"

Croney grinned. "When's the banquet? Am I invited?"

Leon jutted his chin at Croney. "You eat too much."

Croney rubbed his belly. "Well, how about having the wedding banquet here and giving Uncle Kam some business?"

CRONEY gave us some lunch after the rush, so it was close to three when we left the Universal. Leon was in a good mood because he had made twenty-five cash and he felt like spending it. He talked about a stereo at Goodwill for the Baby Store. He was hinting. Leon's ideas were pretty good, but the problem was that he never finished anything he started. And I thought it was a lot of trouble. Did Mah even want a stereo? I told him fixing old things was a headache. But I was wasting my breath; what he enjoys most is making old things work.

We were on Pacific, walking past the red iron gates of the West Ping Projects when someone shouted down at us, *"Wey!* Mr. Walk-Around-in-the-Middle-of-the-Day!"

I looked up and saw Jimmy Lowe.

"Lazy bum," Leon yelled back. "I'm retired. I'm eating social security."

Jimmy Lowe waved from the emerald-painted balcony, "Wait, I come down. Tell you some news."

Leon bellowed back, "Your news is dragged in from the bottom of the sea!"

Yelling in the street! I was embarrassed.

Jimmy Lowe slipped through the iron gates. He turned a quick shoulder down and lowered his voice, still chewing on a toothpick. I knew the pose: committee talk, another get-rich scheme. Leon leaned closer, interested.

I shifted from one foot to the other. Great, I thought, so Leon is hanging around with Chinatown drift-abouts. Spitters. Sitters. Flea men in the Square. Mah calls Jimmy Lowe the Mo-yeah-do-Bak (Mr. Have-Nothing-to-Do). Most of the old guys have nothing to do, but Jimmy Lowe has less to do than any of them. Mah never liked the guy. When we had the grocery store, Jimmy was always coming by and sitting around for hours. He hasn't changed; he uses the Baby Store in the same way. I was just about to tell Leon that I'd meet him there when

I heard him talking about me and Mason getting married in New York.

"Lucky for you! Happy for you!" Jimmy Lowe slapped Leon's back.

"Okay. Next time we talk. We go now to see Mason, my son-in-law." Leon winked at me. "Right?"

I nodded, glad it wasn't only the twenty-five dollars and the thought of another project that put Leon in a good mood. He was happy for Mason and me.

Crossing Kearney, Leon said, "Poor Jimmy Lowe. Got nothing better to do than to cook up schemes."

But wasn't going to see Mason a clever scheme? Goodwill was in the Mission, near Mason's shop—Leon figured he'd have time to hunt around for some junk before Mason got off. I thought, why not? We had a couple of hours before dinner, and besides, I was looking for some time out myself. I wasn't ready to tell Mah the news.

UP BROADWAY I drove fast, made every light: Grant, Stockton, Powell. No stops, a straight shot through the tunnel; Mason would've been proud. Just before moving into the shadow that led us out of Chinatown, we passed the Edith Eaton school. I work there. Five days a week I pass this spot.

Next to the school is the Nam Ping Yuen, the last of the four housing projects built in Chinatown. *Nam* means south and *ping yuen*—if you want to get into it—is something like "peaceful gardens." We call it the Nam. I've heard other names: The Last Ping. The Fourth Ping. For us, the Nam is a bad-luck place, a spooked spot.

My middle sister, Ona, jumped off the M floor of the Nam. The police said she was on downers. But I didn't translate that for Mah or tell her everything else I heard, because by then I was all worn-out from dealing with death in two languages. I knew Ona was doing ludes, but I'd gone through a downer stage myself, so I didn't worry. I was trying to break away from always being the Big Sister. And I really couldn't blame her for doing all that stuff and keeping quiet. Those days, Mah and Leon were giving her a hard time for going out with Osvaldo.

After Ona jumped, Mah was real messed up. She didn't think it was a thing to be gotten over. "Better a parent before a child, better a wife than a husband," she cried. "Everything's all turned around, all backward." Mah wanted to live with it and so we all did for a while. We lived with the ghost, the guilt. But then it got too dark.

Like that, we all just snapped apart. For me, it was as if time broke down: Before and After Ona Jumped. I didn't want anything to be the same. I wanted a new life, as if to say that person then, that person that wasn't able to save Ona, that person was not me. All of us took that trip, but we came back to ourselves, to our old ways. I had to believe that it'd been Ona's choice.

Ona has become a kind of silence in our lives. We don't talk about her. We don't have anything more to say.

I always thought Nina had the best deal because she escaped the day-to-day of it: the every-single-moment. She got time away from the fright of it; and to me, that was being free. But on this trip to New York, I saw different, I saw that Nina still suffered.

I CAUGHT a quick tangy whiff. Leon peeled a tangerine and handed me a slice. I popped the segment, its tart taste bursting in my mouth.

Having Leon in the car with me made it feel like a regular workday. I just started my new position as the community relations specialist for my school, and I do a lot of home visits. I've taken Leon along a couple of times. I told him I needed the company so that he'd think he was doing me a favor—the truth was I hated the thought of him hanging around with those fleabags at Portsmouth Square every single day.

My job is about being the bridge between the classroom teacher and the parents. Teachers target the kids, and I make home visits; sometimes a student needs special tutoring, sometimes it's a disciplinary problem I have to discuss with the parents. My job is about getting the parents involved, opening up a line of communication. I speak enough Chinese and I'm pretty good with parents, but it still surprises me how familiar some of the frustration still feels. The job sounds great on paper, but sometimes, when I'm face to face with the parent, I get this creepy feeling that I'm doing a bit of a missionary number.

Most of my students are recent immigrants. Both parents work. Swing shift. Graveyard. Seamstress. Dishwasher. Janitor. Waiter. One job bleeds into another. They have enough worries, and they don't like me coming in and telling them they have one more.

I invite them to the parent-teacher meetings, the annual potluck. At the evaluation conferences, I tell them that their participation is important.

They tell me, "That's your job. In China, the teacher bears all responsibility."

I use my This Isn't China defense. I remind them "We're in America." But some parents take this to heart and raise their voices. "We're Chinese first, always." I can't win an argument in Chinese and I've learned from experience to stop the argument right there, before I lose all my authority.

Being inside their cramped apartments depresses me. I'm reminded that we've lived like that, too. The sewing machine next to the television, the rice bowls stacked on the table, the rolled-up blankets pushed to one side of the sofa. Cardboard boxes everywhere, rearranged and used as stools or tables or homework desks. The money talk at dinnertime, the list of things they don't know or can't figure out. Cluttered rooms. Bare lives. Every day I'm reminded nothing's changed about making a life or raising kids. Everything is hard.

What's hard for me is realizing that the parents seem more in need than the kids. They try too hard, and it's all wrong; they overdo the politeness and their out-of-context compliments grate on my nerves. "You're so Chinese. You're so smart. You should run for Miss Chinatown."

I try to tell them I can't take the full responsibility for the education of their children. But they keep on with their beliefs. "You're the teacher. Hit them if they don't obey. Scold them till they learn."

After they stuff oranges into my book bag, they ask their favors. Time is what they want. A minute. A call to the tax man, a quick letter to the unemployment agency. I do what I can. What's an extra hour?

Growing up, I wasn't as generous. I hated standing in the lines: social security, disability, immigration. What I hated most was the talking for Mah and Leon, the whole translation number. Every English word counted and I was responsible. I went through a real resentment stage. Every English word was like a curse. I'm over that now, I think.

Thinking about all this overwhelmed me. I hadn't had a minute to myself since coming home; I needed time. I didn't want to rummage through a smelly secondhand store; I didn't want to walk over passed-out drunks. Goodwill was the last place I wanted to go; good will was the last thing I felt. So I dropped my problem parent off. "Just look," I told him. "Don't buy."

I had about an hour before Mason got off work, so I just cruised around, trying to work up the courage to tell Mah that I'd gotten married without talking to her first. This wasn't the first time I'd done something and not told. I have a whole different vocabulary of feeling in English than in Chinese, and not everything can be translated.

For me, the one good thing about getting married was that I was finally rid of my real father's name. Fu. I've always hated its sound. *Fu* in our dialect sounds like the word for bitter.

I'm not deaf; Leila Louie isn't a winning combination either. But I didn't get married just for a name change. I wanted a marriage of choice. I wanted this marriage to be for me.

For a long time, I resisted marriage, but I don't want to get into that now. What I wanted to say to Mah was this: Have a heart, show some compassion. My way wasn't exactly fun. Last minute, like refugees, a strange city. Hurried. A borrowed dress. No rings. Just yes, yes.

WHEN I drove back to Goodwill, Leon was already outside, waiting. I saw the black boxes from a distance. Leon smiled sheepishly and climbed in, carrying a scratched-up speaker in each arm.

I said in an exasperated tone, "Told you not to buy anything!" I hate it when I get bitchy like that, but once I'm in the mood, I can't stop. Mason hates it, too. He says my anger is like flooding—too much gas, killing the engine.

Mason noticed right away that I was upset when I picked him up at the garage. He told me to relax; he shook my knee. "It doesn't matter. Leon just wants to have something to give Mah," he said.

I like that about Mason. He's generous and he can let something go. Sure, I went for Mason for his looks, his long, lean build and his car. But he's got plenty of other qualities: he has a job and he finishes whatever he starts.

"Hey," Mason said, "when are you going to tell your Mah?"

Just then, I had a great idea. I said, "How about *you* telling her?" It was perfect. Mah wouldn't get mad at Mason; he's the son she never had.

Here was the thought that turned everything around: It was Mason Louie I married. We didn't speak the same dialect, but he was one of us.

One truth opened another. Ona still shaded everything we did. Ona's death was the last family affair. I'd seen Mah suffer. I'd seen her break. Now more than anything, I wanted to see her happy.

I thought about it as we circled twice around Stockton Street and I decided the best thing to do was to get out first and go talk to Mah. I suggested parking at the Vallejo Street lot; but I'd forgotten Mason's rule, his commandment: In Chinatown, he never pays to park.

I told Leon I was going to the Baby Store to tell Mah the news. "You want to come?"

He shook his head. "Good luck." He smiled and said, "Tell her it's good luck for us. We have a son now."

EVERYTHING had an alert quality. Brisk wind, white light. I turned down Sacramento and walked down the hill at a snap-quick pace toward Mah's Baby Store.

Mason was the one who started calling it the Baby Store, and the name just stuck. The old sign with the characters for "Herb Shop" still hangs precariously above the door. I've offered to take it down for Mah, but she's said No every time. Mason thinks she wants to hide.

An old carousel pony with a gouged eye and chipped tail stands in front of the store like a guard looking out onto Grant Avenue. I tapped it as I walked past, my quick good-luck stroke. A string of bells jingled as I pushed through the double doors.

A bitter ginseng odor and a honeysuckle balminess greeted me. Younger, more Americanized mothers complain that the baby clothes have absorbed these old world odors. They must complain about how old the place looks, too, with the custom-made drawers that line the wall from floor to ceiling, the factory lighting. Leon wanted to tear down the wall of mahogany drawers and build a new storage unit. But Mah doesn't want him touching anything in her store, and I was glad, too, because I love the tuck-perfect fit of the drawers, and the *tock!* sound the brass handles make against the hard wood.

Mah was showing off her newest stock of jackets to a woman and her child. I gave a quick nod and went straight to the back, where the boxes were stacked two-high. The fluorescent lights glowed, commercial bright.

The woman tried to bargain the price down but Mah wouldn't budge; she changed the subject. "Your girl is very pretty. How about I don't charge tax?"

Hearing that gave me courage. Mah was in a generous, no-tax mood, and that gave me high hopes for some kind of big discount, too. I knew I'd be tongue-tied soon, so I tried to press my worry down by telling myself what Grandpa Leong used to tell me, that the best way to conquer fear is to act.

Open the mouth and tell.

As soon as the woman and her child walked out the door, I went up to Mah and started out in Chinese, "I want to tell you something."

Mah looked up, wide-eyed, expectant.

I switched to English, "Time was right, so Mason and I just went to City Hall. We got married there."

Mah's expression didn't change.

"In New York," I said.

No answer.

"You know I never liked banquets, all that noise and trouble. And such a waste of so much money."

She still didn't say anything. Suddenly I realized how quiet it was, and that we were completely alone in the store. I heard the hum of the lights.

"Mah?" I said. "Say something."

She didn't even look at me, she just walked away. She went to the back of the store and ripped open a box. I followed and watched her bend the flaps back and pull out armfuls of baby clothes. I waited. She started stacking little mounds. She smoothed out sleeves on top of sleeves, zipped zippers, and cupped the colored hoods, one into another. All around our feet were tangles of white hangers.

"Nina was my witness." My voice was whispery, strange.

Mah grunted, a huumph sound that came out like a curse. My translation was: Disgust, anger. There's power behind her sounds. Over the years I've listened and rendered her Chinese grunts into English words.

She threw the empty box on the floor and gave it a quick kick.

"Just like that.
Did it and didn't tell.
Mother Who Raised You.
Years of work, years of worry.
Didn't! Even! Tell!"

WHAT could I say? Using Chinese was my undoing. She had a world of words that were beyond me.

Mah reached down and picked up a tangle of hangers. She poked them into the baby down coats, baby overalls, baby sleepers. Her wrists whipped back and forth in a way that reminded me of how she used to butcher birds on Salmon Alley. Chickens, pheasants, and pigeons, once a frog. The time with the frog was terrible. Mah skinned it and then stopped. She held the twitching muscle out toward us; she wanted us to see its pink heart. Her voice was spooky, breathless: "Look how the heart keeps beating!" Then the frog sprang out of her hand, still vigorous.

Now I said in English, "It was no big deal."

"It is!"

Mah was using her sewing-factory voice, and I remembered her impatience whenever I tried to talk to her while she was sewing on a deadline.

She rapped a hanger on the counter. "Marriage is for a lifetime, and it should be celebrated! Why sneak around, why act like a thief in the dark?"

I wanted to say: I didn't marry in shame. I didn't marry like you. Your marriages are not my fault. Don't blame me.

Just then the bells jingled and I looked up and saw two sewing ladies come through the door. I recognized the round hair, the hawk eyes. ·

"What?" I was too upset to stop. "What?" I demanded again. "You don't like Mason, is that it?"

"Mason," Mah spoke his name soft, "I love."

For love, she used a Chinese word: to embrace, to hug.

I stepped around the boxes, opened my arms and hugged Mah. I held her and took a deep breath and smelled the dried honeysuckle stems, the bitter ginseng root. Above us, the lights beamed bright.

I heard the bells jingle, the latch click, and looked up to see the broad backs of the ladies going out the door toward Grant Avenue. They were going to Portsmouth Square, and I knew they were talking up everything they heard, not stopping when they passed their husbands by the chess tables, not stopping until they found their sewing-lady friends on the benches of the lower level. And that's when they'd tell, tell their long-stitched version of the story, from beginning to end.

Let them make it up, I thought. Let them talk.

TWO

AFTER Ona died, Leon and Mah acted as if all they heard were their own hearts howling. I felt lost between his noisy loneliness and her endless lament. And I knew Mason wasn't liking that I was staying on Salmon Alley and only visiting him on weekends.

Nina came through for me. She was already living in New York, working as a flight attendant, and she offered to take Mah to Hong Kong. She thought that Leon and Mah just needed a break from each other. It was Mah's first trip back. When she left Hong Kong, everyone called her lucky; to live in America was to have a future.

Secretly I was glad I didn't have to go. I felt for Mah; I felt her shame and regret, to go back for solace and comfort, instead of offering banquets and stories of the good life. Twenty-five years in the land of gold and good fortune, and then she returned to tell her story: the years spent in sweatshops, the prince of the Golden Mountain turned into a toad, and three daughters: one unmarried, another who-cares-where, one dead. I could hear the hushed tone of their questions: "Why? What happened? Too sad!"

The generational contact was a comfort to Mah, and Nina even met a Chinese guy who offered her a job as a tour guide. So they should have come back relieved and renewed. But I don't know what got into Nina, why she had to tell them about the abortion she'd had. I didn't see what good it would do, telling, but Nina did.

Mah and Leon joined forces and ganged up on her, said awful things, made her feel like she was a disgrace. Nina was rotten, doomed, no-good. Good as dead. She'd die in a gutter without rice in her belly, and her spirit—if she had one—wouldn't be fed. They forecast bad days in this life and the next. They used a word that sounded like *dyeen*. I still can't find an exact translation, but in my mind it's come to mean something lowly, despised.

"I have no eyes for you," Mah said.

"Don't call us," Leon said.

I knew they were using Nina to vent their own frustration and anger about Ona's suicide. I still wonder if there wasn't another way. Everything about that time was steamy and angry. There didn't seem to be any answers.

Of course they hit on me, too: I was the eldest; they thought I was responsible. "You should have known. You should have said something, done something." What could I have said? Don't sleep with him? Find a Chinese guy at least? Like with Ona, I figured it was her own choice.

That's what this trip is about. I want another kind of relationship with Nina. I want an intimacy with her I hadn't had with Ona the last few years.

Nina and I are half-sisters. I have another father and almost eight years over her, but it's not time that separates us, it's temperament. I could endure; I could shut my heart and let Mah and Leon rant. Nina couldn't. She yelled back. She said things. She left.

Being alone and so far away wasn't easy on Nina. She finally quit because flying made her feel like Leon. "Now I understood why he was so out of it. He was always pushing through another time zone."

Nina didn't want to come back to San Francisco. She

took a job taking tours to China even though she'd never been to China.

THE DAY Mason and I flew into Kennedy, Nina had just returned from a tour along the Yangtze. Mason knew I had family stuff to talk to her about so he went to Brooklyn to see some guys he knew from mechanic school. Nina was still on China time and she wanted to eat early.

When I suggested Chinatown, Nina said it was too depressing. "The food's good," she said, "but the life's hard down there. I always feel like I should rush through a rice plate and then rush home to sew culottes or assemble radio parts or something."

I agreed. At Chinatown places, you can only talk about the bare issues. In American restaurants, the atmosphere helps me forget. For my reunion with Nina, I wanted nice light, handsome waiters, service. I wanted to forget about Mah and Leon.

"I don't want to eat guilt," Nina said. "Let's splurge. My treat. I made great tips this trip. Besides, I've had Chinese food for twenty-seven days."

We were early and the restaurant wasn't crowded. Our waiter was Spanish and he had that dark island tone Nina likes. I noticed him looking Nina up and down as we walked in. Nina saw, I'm sure, but it didn't bother her. I watched her hold his look while she ordered two Johnnie Walkers. When he strutted off, she said, "Cute."

"Tight ass."

"The best."

The place was called The Santa Fe and it was done in peach and cactus green. I looked down at the black plates on the pale tablecloth and thought, Ink. I felt strange. I didn't know this tablecloth, this linen, these candles. Everything seemed foreign. It felt like we should be different people. But each time I looked up, she was the same. I knew her. She was my sister. We'd sat with chopsticks, mismatched bowls, braids, and braces, across the Formica tabletop.

Nina picked up her fork and pressed her thumb against the sharp points. "I like three-pronged forks," she said. "It's funny, but you know I hardly ever use chopsticks anymore. At home I eat my rice on a plate, with a fork. I only used chopsticks to hold my hair up." She laughed, tossed her head back. It was Leon's laugh. "Now I have no use for them at all."

I couldn't help it; I rolled my eyes. Who did she think she was talking to, some rich matron lady cruising the Yangtze?

No more braids. In Hong Kong this last trip, she'd cut her hair very short and it showed off her finely shaped head.

I asked if she remembered when Leon gave her a boy's haircut.

Nina looked worried and she touched her head lightly. "Do I look like that, now?"

"No, you look great."

Her hair used to fall down wild to her waist. Nina had Mah's hair: thick and dark and coarse, hair that braids like rope. Now Nina was all features, a brush of brow, long eyes, a slender neck. She looked more vulnerable.

Nina is reed thin and tall. She has a body that clothes look good on. Nina slips something on and it wraps her like skin. Fabric has pulse on her.

In high school, Chinese guys who liked Nina but were afraid to ask her out spread a rumor that she only went out with white guys. When Nina heard about it, she found out which guys and went up to each one of them and told them off.

Nina talked about China, how strange it felt to see only Chinese people. She liked Zhang, the national guide assigned to her group. He spoke Spanish. She was lucky, she said. Zhang was usually assigned to the European tours. She was the first overseas Chinese he'd met. He showed her around Canton; he knew it well; he'd been there during the Cultural Revolution. She was impressed when he brought out his guitar and played Spanish flamenco for the variety show. Nina said, "I like Zhang. He's different."

Everything struck me as strange: Nina saying Guangzhou, Shanghai, Xian, and Chengdu in the northern dialect, Nina in China, Nina with a Chinese guy.

I thought about our different worlds now: Nina had a whole map of China in her head; I had Chinatown, the Mission, the Tenderloin.

Going to China had helped Nina make up with Mah and Leon. When Nina passed through SFO to pick up passengers on her first China trip, Mah and Leon had been too excited to hold on to the grudge. They wanted to go to the airport and see Nina as she changed planes. Mah and Leon and Nina had a reconciliation walking from Domestic to International.

"Are you thinking of marrying this Zhang guy to get him out?" I asked.

Nina said she wasn't stupid and then she turned the question on me, "So, what's your problem with marrying?"

I shrugged. "The banquets. I always hated them."

Nina agreed. "All those people."

We remembered feeling out of place at the huge Leong banquets. Leon and Mah, Ona, Nina, and I, we counted five, one hand, but seated around the banquet table, we barely made a half-circle. We looked for the cute guys, hoping one would be assigned to our table, but we always got the strays: an out-of-town relative, an old man, a white person.

I looked around the restaurant. The waiters were lighting candles. Our waiter brought the drinks. He stopped very close to Nina, seemed to breathe her in. When Nina turned her face toward him I saw the reddish highlights in her hair. We ordered, and the waiter moved off into the dark again.

My scotch tasted good. It reminded me of Leon, Johnnie Walker, or Seagram's 7, that's what they served at Chinese banquets. Nine courses and a bottle. Leon taught us how to drink it from the teacups, without ice. He drank his from a rice bowl, sipping it like hot soup. But by the end of the meal he took it like cool tea, in bold mouthfuls. Nina, Ona, and I, we sat watching, our teacups of scotch in our laps, his three giggly girls.

Relaxed, I thought there was a connection. Johnnie Walker then and Johnnie Walker now. I twirled the glass to make the ice tinkle.

We clinked glasses. Three times for good luck. I relaxed, felt better.

"What's going on with you and Mason?"

"He wants to get married."

"Isn't it about time?"

"I guess." I wasn't in the mood to talk about it yet. "Here's to Johnnie Walker in shark's fin soup," I said.

"And squab dinners."

"I Love Lucy." I raised my glass, and said again, "To *I Love Lucy*, squab dinners, and brown bags."

"To bones."

"Bones," I repeated. This was a funny that got sad, and knowing it, I kept laughing. I was surprised how much memory there was in one word. Pigeons. Only recently did I learn that the name for them was squab. Our name for them was pigeon—on a plate or flying over Portsmouth Square. A good meal at forty cents a bird. In line by dawn, we waited at the butcher's, listening for the slow, churning motor of the trucks. We watched the live fish flushing out of the tanks into the garbage pails. We smelled the honey-brushed *cha-sui* buns. And when the white laundry truck turned into Wentworth Alley with its puffing trail of feathers, a stench of chicken waste and rotting food filled the alley. Old ladies squeezed in around the truck, reaching into the crates to tug out the plumpest pigeons.

Nina, Ona, and I picked the white ones, those with the most expressive eyes. Dove birds, we called them. We fed them leftover rice in water, and as long as they stayed plump, they were our pets, our baby dove birds.

But then one day we'd come home from school and find them cooked. Mah said they were special, a nutritious treat. She filled our bowls high with little pigeon parts: legs, breasts, and wings. She let us take our dinners out to the front room to watch *I Love Lucy*. Mah opened up a brown bag for the bones. We leaned forward, balanced our bowls on our laps, and crossed our chopsticks in midair and laughed at Lucy. We called out, "Mah! Mah! Come watch! Watch Lucy cry!"

But Mah always sat alone in the kitchen sucking out the

sweetness of the lesser parts: the neck, the back, and the head. "Bones are sweeter than you know," she always said. She came out to check the bag. "Clean bones." She shook it. "No waste."

OUR dinners came with a warning: "Don't touch. Enjoy." The waiter smiled at Nina but she kept her head down.

I couldn't remember how to say "scallops" in Chinese. Nina shrugged; she didn't know either.

She asked, "What's going on with them? Are they getting along?"

Nina knew I was thinking about Mah and Leon. It's true what Leon says, Nina has radar that way. But I could tell Nina had to work herself up to even mention them, so it's also true what Mah says, that Nina wants the family to be the last thing on her mind. But I didn't hold back, I told her I'd come to New York to get away from their bickering.

"The lights," I said. "At the store. Leon left the job half done. Mah was working in the dark. She called him a useless thing, a stinking corpse. And Leon had an answer. You know that fortune teller's voice he uses when he's on the edge, like he's giving warning? Well, he swore to jump from the Golden Gate, told her not to bother with burying him because even when dead he wouldn't be far enough away. And then he used that stupid thousand-year-old curse of his, you know that one, something about damning the good will that blinded him into taking her as his wife."

Nina speared a scallop and put it on my plate. "Eat," she said. She speared another and ate.

My eyes narrowed; I gave her a serious Big Sister look. "You know what the Baby Store is for Mah . . ."

Something about Nina's expression made me stop: how her eyes flinched, sudden, and how her lips made a contorting line, as if she tasted something bitter.

For a moment, I wanted to force it on her: He's your father.

She couldn't even look at me. She didn't want to hear it. She said I was always telling stories the way she couldn't stand to hear. She thought I had the peace of heart, knowing I'd done my share for Mah and Leon. And I thought she had the courage of heart, doing what she wanted.

I thought about how we were sisters. We ate slowly, chewing like old people; it was a way to fool the stomach, our way of making things last. I speared one of my prawns and put it on her plate. "Try," I said.

The waiter came and asked if everything was all right.

"Everything," Nina said.

I watched him watch Nina. Another time, he might've been lucky. He was definitely her type, a Fa-fa prince, a flower picker, like my father.

She looked up, smiled. The light from the candle made her eyes shimmer. Nina had Mah's eyes. Eyes that made you want to talk.

"I just don't want it," I said.

"Want what?" Nina asked.

"The banquet and stuff."

"You don't have to."

"Mah wants it."

"So?"

"So what am I supposed to say? Mah wants one. She has obligations."

"What are you talking about?"

I put my fork down. "Everybody's always inviting her to their banquets, and she's never had the occasion to invite back."

Nina's voice got harder. "Now you're thinking like her."

"Like what?"

"Do it the way you want."

"It's not that easy."

We didn't say anything for a while. We chewed.

Finally Nina said, "Yes, it is."

I couldn't think of anything to say. I'd already had this argument with Mason too many times. I wanted to say it was easy for her to talk, being three thousand miles away.

But Nina's voice went soft. "Look, you've always been on standby for them. Waiting and doing things their way. Think about it, they have no idea what our lives are about. They don't want to come into our worlds. We keep on having to live in their world. They won't move one bit."

She looked straight at me. "I know about it, too. I helped fill out those forms at the Chinatown employment agencies; I went to the Seaman's Union, too; I listened and hoped for those calls: 'Busboy! Presser! Prep man!' And I know about *should.* I know about *have to.* We should. We want to do more, we want to do everything. But I've learned this: I *can't.*"

"Listen." Nina leaned forward. "Marry Mason here. Marry Mason now."

The waiter came by to ask about dessert. Nina shook her head, said she knew a better place.

Nina was right. Mah's and Leon's lives were always on high fire. They both worked too hard; it was as if their marriage was a marriage of toil—of toiling together. The idea was that the next generation would marry for love. The old way. Matches were made, strangers were wedded, and that was fate. Marriage was for survival. Men were scarce: dead from the wars, or working abroad as sojourners. As such, my father, Lyman Fu, was considered a prince. Mah married my father to escape the war-torn villages, and when he ran off on her, she married Leon to be saved from disgrace.

Saved to work. Mah sat down at her Singer with the dinner rice still in her mouth. When we pulled down the Murphy bed, she was still there, sewing. The hot lamp made all the stitches blur together; the street noises stopped long before she did. And in the morning, long before any of us awoke, she was already there, at work.

Leon worked hard, too. Out at sea, on the ships, Leon worked every room: Engine, Deck, and Navigation. He ran the L. L. Grocery while holding down a night job as a welder at the Bethlehem Steel yard. He talked about a Chinese takeout, a noodle factory, many ideas. Going into the partnership with Luciano Ong was the first real thing that looked promising, but then it went dangerously the other way.

We remembered how good Mah was to him. How else would we have known him all those years he worked on the ships? Mah always gave him majestic welcomes home, and it was her excitement that made us remember him.

I know Leon, how ugly his words could become. I've heard him. I've listened. And I've always wished for the street noises, as if in the traffic of sound I could escape. I know the hard color of his eyes and the tightness in his jaw. I can almost hear his teeth grind. I know this. Years of it.

Their lives weren't easy. So is their discontent without reason?

What about the first one? You didn't even think to come to the hospital. The first one, I say! Son or daughter, dead or alive, you didn't even come!

What about living or dying? Which did you want for me that time you pushed me back to work before my back brace was off?

Money! Money!! Money to eat with, to buy clothes with, to pass this life with!

Don't start that again! Everything I make at that dead place I hand . . .

How come . . .
What about . . .
So . . .

How many times have Nina, Ona, and I held them apart? The flat *ting!* sound as the blade slapped onto the linoleum floor, the wooden handle of the knife slamming into the corner. Which one of us screamed, repeating all their ugliest words? Who shook them? Who made them stop?

It was obvious. The stories themselves meant little. It was how hot and furious they could become.

Is there no end to it? What makes their ugliness so alive, so thick and impossible to let go of?

WE'RE lucky, not like the bondmaids growing up in service, or the newborn daughters whose mouths were stuffed with ashes. The beardless, soft-shouldered eunuchs, the courtesans with the three-inch feet and the frightened child brides—they're all stories to us. Nina, Ona, and I, we're the lucky generation. Mah and Leon forced themselves to live through the humiliation in this country so that we could have it better. We know so little of the old country. We repeat the names of grandfathers and uncles, but they have always been strangers to us. Family exists only because somebody has a story, and knowing the story connects us to a history. To us, the deformed man is oddly compelling, the forgotten man is a good story, and a beautiful woman suffers.

THE WAITER stood there, the dark plates balanced on his arm.

"You two Chinese?" he asked.

"No." I let my irritation fill the word. "We're two sisters."

MASON and I only paid five dollars to get married at City Hall. The dark-suited man who married us had the distracted expression of a sweatshop presser. We had just enough time to say I do.

The day was overcast. It was late enough in the afternoon to think about dinner and we decided on Chinatown because it was close enough to walk to. We walked past food carts and I saw the vendors frying dumplings, flipping tofu squares. I liked the urgent, time-pressed feeling on wide Canal Street, the honking cabs, the line of trucks moving like thick ink toward the Manhattan Bridge. Shoppers and sightseers. No strollers, everyone was in a hurry.

We stopped to watch a man pulling threadlike strands between his outstretched hands. Nina said he was counting to a thousand.

"Dragon whiskers," she said. "Candy. A Hong Kong treat."

We bought three. The fine-combed squares melted in our mouths. Sweet. Sticky. A sesame taste.

Nina said she felt rain coming on.

"Great. Rain means good luck."

THREE

WE WERE at Mason's place, downstairs in the garage. Zeke Louie (no relation) was downtown picking up an alternator, so I sat in the jacked-up BMW waiting for Mason to say when; I was helping bleed the brakes. It was Mason's cousin's car, and Mason was finishing work on it. He wanted to deliver it to Redwood City the next day, Sunday. We had an early flight to New York on Monday. Time was pretty tight.

Mason took extra care with this job, not for his cousin Dale, who he thought was a jerk, but for his Aunt Lily, who Mason said was good to his family when they were growing up in Chinatown.

This time, Zeke really came through for Mason. He's the body man at Phaedrus, the BMW shop on Van Ness, and he arranged it so Mason could work on the car there all day Friday. That made tuning it a breeze, using the high-class equipment. Zeke showed me around when I dropped lunch off, and I was really impressed: all the mechanics wore white shirts.

Mason was a little bummed out because he'd just heard that he didn't get the call for the job at the Audi shop. Mason's a good mechanic—foreign cars only. I told him that he should set up his own business. Maybe, he said, maybe with Zeke. I thought he was good enough to go it alone. Zeke's his oldest friend and Mason's loyal to that. Mason believes that time would be the guarantee; the years they'd known each other would count and everything they went through would matter.

Sure, I agreed Zeke was an old friend, but old doesn't necessarily make good when it comes to partnerships. I wanted to say something about Zeke's temper, but I held my tongue. It wasn't my place to talk; it was their business. I had to leave some things alone.

"Now," Mason said.

I gave the pedal six pumps.

"Again."

I pumped again.

"All right."

"How much longer?" I wanted to know. I still had to pack.

"One more time should do it."

I pumped again. Mason was saying something, so I got out of the car and went around to the back.

"I forgot . . ." His voice seemed to be coming from the other side of a tunnel, from a long way off. "Your Mah called yesterday, when you were shopping."

I heard a grunt, a clank, a release of air. Mason rolled out from underneath and jumped to his feet. He brushed the loose strands off his face. His dark blue work suit was stained with oil. "Done."

"What she want?"

Mason shrugged. "Just lonely, I think. She just wanted to talk." He opened the garage door and I went out and stood in the street, watching him. Mason had a smooth way of moving; he could dip and slide under a car, lean over and reach halfway into the engine, and never lose his balance. He hardly ever slips, even when he's put all his weight into turning a rusted lug nut. Mason is long and lean and I love the way he wears his face, tough and closed to outsiders, but open to me.

The globed street lamps came on and then a white

Mercedes pulled into the driveway. Zeke stepped out carrying the alternator, all excited because he'd gotten a deal on the job. He told me rebuilt was better than new. But he wouldn't say how much he paid. Zeke's rule was that you didn't take money from friends.

"You could take me to dinner sometime." Then he winked at me. "Or you could set me up with Nina."

We laughed about that. Zeke had a longtime crush on Nina. He had that build that she liked—the tight fit of muscle and nerve—but not enough height to carry it off. At fourteen, Nina was already towering over him. Once she said he was too "Chinatown," but that's not something I'd repeat.

Zeke grew up hanging around his uncle's gas station, the one with the "76" sign in Chinese on the corner of Pacific and Taylor. His uncle had Zeke do the detail work, the shine and buff, and now he still calls Zeke the "Detail Man." Some guys still call him Detail, but I like to call him Zeke. His mother'd asked a nurse at Chinese Hospital to give him an American name. Ezekiel was what he got. A spit-quick kind of name. I thought it was perfect; Zeke was a short man with a short temper. With his help, getting the car into shape wasn't going to take much longer.

I went upstairs to call Mah back. She was upset about Nina. She wanted me to tell Nina to come home. I didn't want to hear it. I wasn't going to tell Nina what to do.

Mah followed every word with a sigh. Each word had a fullness that twisted me up inside. Listening, I could see her, the way I saw her so many nights in the dark Salmon Alley apartment, crumpled in her chair, her voice raw, calling for Ona.

Now I wasn't listening. I scraped the dead skin off the

inside-underneath of my nails and I pushed the cuticles back till the moons showed. When Mah used that tone, I tried to stay in the safe and quiet middle.

Through the air vents, I heard clanging and pounding, congratulatory "All rights," and the heavy clang of the hubcaps going back on; the metal sounds had a high final ring.

Mah said something about how everything started with me, since I was the first one, the eldest, the one with the daring to live with Mason when I wasn't married. She said it in that irrational way she has, "That's why Ona went bad. That's why Nina left."

I didn't want to get into a fight before my trip. But I couldn't help saying something and my tone wasn't the kindest. "Nina wanted to go. Don't blame me."

The line clicked twice, then cut. The dial tone had a wide, hollow sound like something heavy sinking slowly. For a minute, I thought to call her back, drive over, and talk to her, but I couldn't face another night on Salmon Alley.

Mason came upstairs to see if I wanted to go on a test run, get something to eat.

"I just talked to Mah. She's upset."

"She's always upset." He was joking, I could tell, but it irritated me a little.

He said, "You think she wants to go for a cruise?"

"Are you kidding?" I shook my head.

Mason reminded me that we were going to be gone early Monday. "There's always something with your Mah." He told me that having the lights put in at the Baby Store and getting Leon signed up for social security were only Band-Aids. The lights didn't pick up business or brighten their marriage, and collecting social security didn't give Leon the feeling of prosperity he needed. Mason gave me his serious look. He said, "Take care of yourself."

I told Mason to go on with Zeke, I felt like staying home and not thinking about anything.

EARLY the next morning, we headed down the peninsula. Zeke and his girlfriend, Diana, followed in the Mercedes so that he could give us a ride back. Mason had the sun roof open, and it felt like we were flying, but I looked over at the speedometer and we were only going seventy. Mason likes to drive fast, not to speed but to sail. But the BMW wasn't his, so he wasn't pushing it. I've always felt safe with him behind the wheel. The best time he made was two and a half hours to Tahoe; I'd helped, checking for helicopters. Being with Mason, being on the road, moving fast in a nice car, I relaxed.

Mason pulled out of his lane, passing Zeke. The BMW leaned and swooped through the hills. The mountains were burnt-orange-colored and then reddish. I buzzed my window down and stuck my head out and took a big gulp of wind. I love wind, especially coastal wind with its salt taste.

White Mercedes. Gold BMW. The two cars kept a close line. But Zeke couldn't take being in the rear too long and he pulled out, passing us, tooting.

Mason shook his head and said, "Can't take being number two."

I reached over and touched Mason's hair. He was wearing it in a tail, his formal look, for the family visit. I liked it better when it was down, long and loose.

Mason said, "How long has it been, this back and forth?"

He meant living on the alley and in the Mission. A reasonable complaint. Mason was clever, the way he asked.

I was clever too. I refused to answer. I was quiet.

He looked over at me but didn't say anything. He only drummed his fingers on the steering wheel.

The car was steady, going fast. Out the window, I saw dry shrubbery, pale sky. I felt the car accelerating; we passed the Mercedes. I felt Mason looking over at me again.

He said, "You have to answer."

I turned and looked at his lean profile. "You want me to move back in with you, is that it?"

Mason drove. He looked at the road, straight ahead. Then he spoke slowly, and his low, steady voice filled the car. He said, "I want you to marry me."

JUST before the Redwood City exit, Mason warned me that if his Aunt Lily wasn't home a half hour was the max he'd stay. He said he couldn't stand talking any longer to Dale. "The guy sounds so white."

It wasn't Dale's fault, but I didn't say anything. Dale grew up on the peninsula and went to an all-white school, so how else was he supposed to talk? I've met a lot of kids like him: fourth-, fifth-, even sixth-generation kids who had no Chinese. To me, they just sounded like English was their only language, nothing wrong with that.

Zeke tooted on the long driveway and Dale came out of the ranch-style house to meet us.

Mason pulled up alongside the Mercedes and got out. He nodded hello and handed Dale the keys.

Dale tossed them in the air. "Thanks, I really appreciate this." He tossed them up again. "What do I owe you?"

"Forget about it."

"No. Really, I'd like to pay you for your time."

Mason had that look on his face, that fuck-this-guy look. I knew that look; it was not good. Money was out of the question. What was this? If money was a question, Dale should've taken it to a shop. Why'd he ask Mason?

But Dale had no clue. He had no idea what was what. He didn't even know that Mason was doing him a family favor.

Dale asked again, but Mason put his hand up, shook his head.

I got worried and started looking around for diversion. I walked over to the glass doors; beyond, I saw the garden, the pool, the lollipop-colored lawn furniture.

Maybe Dale felt the tension rising, maybe he was smarter than I gave him credit for. He offered us something to drink, he invited us to sit by the pool.

"Let's go," Zeke said. "Scotch would be nice."

We followed Dale through the house into the yard. Zeke was impressed with the pool, the view, the leather couch, the scotch. Diana and I had a Coke. Mason wasn't thirsty; he lit a cigarette. I asked how Aunt Lily was. How was the new computer company?

Aunt Lily was working at the Stanford mall. Business was good. I didn't mind him bragging about his successful company, I was just glad someone was talking. Mason was squinting, because he was sitting in the sun. (He did it on purpose; he'd rather look into the sun than at Dale.)

"Sun feels good here." Mason ran his hand through his hair and leaned back; he rocked on the back legs of his chair.

Zeke nodded. He ran his hand through his hair too.

From where I sat, I saw his perm kinking up, I could see the pink of his scalp, the sweat spots.

Mason looks good in the sun. Summer or winter, Mason always looks good. He smells good too. He always has that faint metal smell in his hair.

I put my hand into the water and watched it ripple. Looking at Dale, I thought he looked pretty good, with his surfer's build, his tennis-tanned legs, and his perfect haircut. His house, his business, and even his smooth English all counted for something, but I knew I could never go with a guy like him. A guy with an uncallused smooth palm, a guy with Sunday hands.

Mason finished his cigarette and stood up. Zeke and Diana put their drinks down.

BACK on the freeway, glad to be on our own again, we all relaxed. It sort of pissed me off to see Dale lounging by the pool after Mason'd spent all weekend under his car.

"Dale should have thanked you too, Zeke," I said.

Mason agreed. "For a computer wiz, the guy's sure stupid."

"No manners," Zeke said. "Doesn't know how to treat people."

"Family," I said.

Diana said, "No home education."

Zeke wanted to go out for dinner. I didn't. Going outside of Chinatown with Zeke was never a great idea. The last time, we went to a comedy club on Clement Street and this comic started in on how Chinese people talked funny, that when they said "three" or "five," it sounded like "fee-fie-fo-fum." Zeke'd shot out of his seat, fist up like he was ready to jump onto the stage and fight about it. He'd shouted, "Cut the fucken Chinese jokes."

Later, walking to the car, I'd whispered to Mason, "Can't he even take a joke?" But Mason'd answered, "How many chink jokes do you have to take?"

So I wasn't in the mood to take chances with Zeke now. I suggested going back to Mason's place, cooking together.

Mason didn't say anything else about getting married on the drive back to San Francisco, but I could tell he was thinking about it. I saw it in his face, how he looked away, how his lips held firm, the tight jaw; he was closing off, going inward. But I knew I was safe. I knew he wouldn't say anything while Zeke and Diana were around. Mason's not the type to talk about stuff like that in front of people, even if Zeke is his closest buddy.

I didn't mention it either, but Mason's face gave me warning, and all evening I asked myself why was it so hard to say yes?

It all went back to Ona. When Mah was spooked after Ona died, she asked me to stay with her on Salmon Alley. I told Mason it was temporary. But how much would Mason take? How long would he wait?

I moved back to the alley because Mah couldn't stand living with the question: What could have saved Ona? The blame is what I can't live with; the fear is what I can't get away from.

I ask over and over again: If I'd been living on the Alley, could I have had that talk with Ona? If I'd been living on the Alley, would I have said the right word?

FOUR

EDWARD YEE'S parents had a five-thirty appointment to come by the school and talk about their son. At six, they were still no show. Since it was my first case on the job, I called, ready to offer to go over for a home visit, but there was no answer.

Outside, a thin light lingered. Stockton Street was still crowded with shoppers and I pushed through, glad I'd done my shopping earlier. Mason's favorites were already in my bag: fresh mushrooms, steaks, a Beaujolais. I rushed, taking the shortcut up through Café Alfredo's parking lot to Salmon Alley; I was worried about getting another parking ticket. Mason would kill me; the car was still registered under his name. That morning I'd been running late and couldn't find parking, so I had just pulled it up onto the curb in the alley. I was banking on either Marty Wong or Randy Gin's being on the parking beat. Either one would recognize the Karmann Ghia.

When I got to the top of the hill and climbed over the thick chain, the sky had darkened but the street lamps hadn't come on yet, so I couldn't be sure till I got right up to the car. No ticket.

I RECOGNIZED the biting scent: ginseng. Its bitterness cut through the dark. That the hall lights weren't on made me secretly glad; I could just pick up my stuff and go; I assumed Mah was working late. My old bedroom was a few feet from the front door; I went in and threw my mail, school papers, some clothes, and my makeup into my black bag and zipped it up, started my getting-ready-to-go routine.

I heard a noise from the other end of the apartment, so I called out, "Mah?"

The living room was dark except for a glow from the quiet television. "How come you're sitting in the dark?" My harsh tone surprised me, so I snapped on a light, trying to push the bad feeling away before it settled into the room. The light was one of Leon's inventions. It used to be an old hat tree. He'd attached a fluorescent ring to the top and small colored bulbs to each hook. Mason thought it looked like a dead Christmas tree.

Mah blinked at the sudden light. "Eaten yet?" Her hello.

I mumbled, "We're cooking tonight."

"What?" But she didn't wait for my answer; she was heading toward the kitchen, saying something about a brew she wanted me to drink. "Have yours first; I'll put Mason's in a jar for you to take."

"Steaks," I answered.

"Don't eat American every day," Mah said. "It's not good for you." She listed my old favorites: beef tendons with *fuun* noodles, fatty pork with shrimp paste, sea cucumber. I've complained to Nina about it: How can I tell her my tastes have changed, like everything else? Nina asked me what I expected. "Mah wasn't just talking about food," she said.

"*Boo nai.*" Good for you. Mah handed me a mug. Then her complaints came rushing out of her mouth: "Leon still hasn't fixed the lights. I've been running my business in the dark."

The ginseng brew was as dark as two-day-old tea.

All day I'd been dealing with other people's problems and now I didn't feel like listening to how Leon never finished anything he started. Leon had heard at the Square that fluorescent lights were better than bulbs and he'd suggested them for the Baby Store. Enthusiastic, Mah went with him to Three Star Hardware and chose soft white over bright white. When Leon carried the ladder up from the basement and perched on the top rung to rewire the switches, she held the ladder steady.

Mason called it their first joint project because it was the friendliest thing they'd done together after Leon moved into the San Fran.

I was glad to see Leon escape into a project. After Ona died, Leon still talked up new ideas, but he hardly ever started anything. Working on the lights, Leon seemed almost his old self, not happy but preoccupied. I was hoping he'd see this project through to the end, but half-way through he told Mason that his concentration was gone, that something disconnected between his mind and his heart.

Then, the S.S. *Independent* docked and You Thin Toy drove up to the Baby Store with his overtime splurge: a dollar-green Impala. The two of them were off on a new project: hunting down bargains at the fleamarkets—Cow Palace, Alameda, Berkeley.

"All head and no tail," Mah said. *"Faat moong,"* she accused. It applied, it was true; Leon had become dreamy, lost.

I sipped. My shoulders felt tight, tense. I tried to relax them, but when I turned my head, it felt like someone was stabbing me in the back. Nothing new. For months, I'd had these pains. When they first came, I thought I'd strained my back at school lifting something or chasing kids on yard duty.

But it wasn't that. It was more like in my head. It was being pulled back and forth between Mah and Mason. All that worry about Leon, his lights, his living alone at the San Fran. It was worrying about my new job and parking tickets and the crowds on Stockton Street and seeing Nina in New York. But right then it was mostly Mah's being alone and Mason's waiting for me.

I sipped again: a long bitter taste. And it was Ona. That's the thing that was in my head. Everything went back to Ona. And beyond Ona there was the bad luck that Leon kept talking about. What made Ona do it. Like she had no choice.

Leon blamed himself. He had this crazy idea that our family's bad luck started when he broke his promise to Grandpa Leong. Grandpa Leong was Leon's father only on paper; he sponsored Leon's entry into the country by claiming him as his own son. It cost Leon. Each time he told us, his eyes opened wide like he was hearing the price called out for the first time. "Five thousand American dollars." Of more consequence was the promise to send Grandpa Leong's bones back to China. Leon was away when Grandpa Leong died. Leon worried about the restless bones, and for years, whenever something went wrong— losing a job, losing the bid for the takeout joint, losing the Ong and Leong Laundry—Leon blamed the bones. But in the end the bones remained here.

Then Ona jumped and it was too late. The bones were lost, like Ona was lost. That's why Leon shipped out on a cargo voyage. Cape Horn was as far away as a ship could go. Forty days to the bottom of the world.

Mah thought it was the bad choices she made. My father, Lyman Fu. Her affair with Tommie Hom. She thought all the bad luck started with her.

Nina blamed us, this family. Everybody. Everything. Salmon Alley. The whole place. That's why she's in New York now. Getting pregnant didn't have to be a problem—I told her to keep the abortion a secret. It was her business. Nobody had to know. Telling was her way out. For a long time she didn't call me, and even now she only half tells me what she does, who she sees. I hear it from other people. My own sister. The way I see it, she's afraid to let us know too much. I used to think she was ashamed of us: the way Leon has turned into an old-man bum, and how bitter Mah is now.

Who knows what she thinks of me? Somehow Nina thought the problem was a combination of us together, cooped up on Salmon Alley. We stirred up the bad luck.

I thought I knew Ona. She was the middle girl, the in-between one. I thought she was some kind of blend of Nina and me, but I had no idea it was such a dangerous mix. Now I feel that I should have known, that I should've *said* something that might have anchored her.

Nina gets mad at me when I keep on about it. "Let it go," she said. "Ona had her own life. It was her choice."

Maybe Nina's right. Too much happened on Salmon Alley.

Salmon Alley's always been home. My father lived a short time with Mah in a small one-bedroom overlooking Pacific Avenue. What I remember about that apartment is the traffic sounds and the constant rumble of Tommie Hom's sweatshop downstairs. After my father went to Australia, Mah went downstairs to work. She didn't have any experience, but Tommie was a good teacher. Buttonhole, overlock, hem, straight seam: Mah learned all the machines. I remember hoping she'd marry Tommie, but Leon was the one who asked. For him it was an easy move from the San Fran: two suitcases and a box of radio parts.

When Ona was born, we moved down the alley into another one of Tommie's buildings. The rooftop, with its view of the Bay Bridge, was the best thing about it. Leon was shipping a lot those days and Tommie Hom was still coming around. I think Leon knew.

Leon shipped less and less after Nina was born. For Leon, it was a period of odd jobs and a lot of dream talking. He was a fry cook at Wa-jin's, a busboy at the Waterfront Restaurant by the Wharf, a janitor at a print shop downtown. But Mah was right. Something always went wrong for Leon.

For us, it was strange having Leon around all the time. We weren't sure about Leon on a long-term basis, considering Tommie Hom and everything. We liked Leon the old way: suddenly here, suddenly gone.

I FINISHED the brew in one long swallow. The mug hit the table harder than I intended. The biting taste lingered; I smacked my lips. A cigarette, a jelly bean, that's what I wanted, something to take the taste away. I went over to the sink, rinsed out the mug, and drank some water, but the ginseng flavor seemed to explode, and the bitter taste filled my mouth again.

"I better hurry," I said. Mah handed me Mason's portion of the brew and then she said something else, but I was already going down the hall. I threw the bag over my shoulder, the straps pinched, and I felt the tension in my back again. I heard Mah say something in her concerned tone.

I shook my head and opened the front door. "Nothing. I'll call you before we go to New York." But she followed me down the stairs.

At the landing, I heard kids' voices. The cool air felt good. For a moment, it felt as though nothing had changed. It felt like the old days, when the first dark hour was a time of everybody's coming home, of being hungry and happy, of waiting for the good food we could smell cooking.

I threw my stuff into the car, got in, and started the engine. I rolled down the window. "Go back," I said. "It's cold."

Mah just stood there.

"Go upstairs." I felt like honking the horn at her. But what I said was, "Mason and I will deal with it, we'll fix the lights."

Mah nodded, then she leaned forward and held up a small jar. "For Leon?"

The car window framed her face. I thought about how she waited till the last minute and then she asked softly, because she was afraid I wouldn't do it. She knew I didn't want to be her go-between.

She asked again. "He's right on your way."

I looked at her wild, perm-damaged hair. I imagined her walking to the San Fran, knocking on Leon's door.

I tried to smile. "Sure, Mah."

Leon's jar of ginseng made a warm circle in my palm, on my lap. I drove to the hotel and parked in the bus zone. Leon was out, so I left the jar at the front desk with Manager Lee.

That night, I moved first. I kissed the hollow of Mason's throat, I licked his smooth lobe. Mason followed, urgent. Like that, moving with Mason, I felt safe.

What do you want? What do you want?

Our question moved between us.

What I wanted was to forget. The blame. The pressing fear. I wanted a ritual that forgave. I wanted a ritual to forget.

MASON offered to put the lights in, so we drove down to the Baby Store early the next morning. It was not yet eight, but all along Stockton Street the trucks were already double-parked, unloading: live fish, vegetables, slabs of beef, and whole pigs. Mason pulled the Camaro right up onto the sidewalk on Grant Avenue. We both went in. Mason dragged the ladder to the center of the store and I pulled the tubes out of the corrugated casings and handed them up to Mason; they lifted away from my hands, as thin as eggshells. Mason snapped them into place, one, two, three.

What was wrong with Leon, leaving the easiest part till last and then walking away?

I flipped the switch, looked up. The white line of lights flickered and snapped and shot across the ceiling, jagged as a headache.

FIVE

LEON needed money coming in if he wanted to continue living at the San Fran. "Social security," I suggested. "Retirement."

Leon didn't like the word and gave me his noncommittal shrug. He said, "I'll wait and just see."

I knew he was holding off because he was still hoping to land that perfect job, find that perfect business. For Leon, taking social security was something like giving up his shipping card. So I did some research and found out he could still work as long as his earnings didn't go over six thousand a year. When I told Leon, I tried to make it sound like a fantastic deal. He could take an occasional odd job and still collect from the government. Leon saw it as an opportunity, a loophole; he agreed to put in his application.

Getting him to say yes was the painless part. I told the school I'd be an hour late at the most, definitely in time for the first recess. But I was at the Van Ness office the whole morning. I wouldn't have minded so much if we'd at least been able to get the application processed.

Leon was always getting his real and paper birthdates mixed up; he's never given the same birthdate twice. Old-timer logic: If you don't tell the truth, you'll never get caught in a lie. What Leon didn't know, he made up. Forty years of making it up had to backfire sometime.

It happened when I took Leon to the social security office. It was as if all the years of work didn't count.

I felt sorry for the interviewer, a young white guy, kind of cute but shy, as though this were his first day on his first job. He was polite, and patient. He asked Leon why he had so many aliases? So many different dates of birth? Did he have a passport? A birth certificate? A driver's license?

Leon had nothing but his anger, and like a string of firecrackers popping, he started cursing.

"Iiiinamahnagahgoddammcocksucksonnahvabitch!"

I mean, *who* could understand it?

When I figured out that Leon picked up his English from shipmates, that the cursing was a replay of how those guys cursed him out, it depressed me even more. Hearing Leon use English just makes me feel bitter.

There was nothing to do but wait, let his long steam blow itself out. Then, as if it were proof, Leon flashed first his driver's license (expired) and then his social security card. His tone was final, "I be in this country long time!"

"Leon," I said, "sit down."

Leon sat down. "People be the tell me. I never talk English good. Them tell me."

"Who told you?" the interviewer asked.

"Them tell me."

"Them?" I lost it when I heard that word. I yelled, "Who? Who!" It drove me crazy the way Leon said it, like finding someone to blame was an answer. I said, "This is fucked. The way you do things is fucked."

Leon shut his face; he wouldn't look at me. I saw him grinding his jaw.

The interviewer just sat there, looking at us, drop-jawed. I started thinking about what other people thought, what they saw: this Chinese girl yelling at her old man. I told myself that Leon would get over it. But I was grateful when the guy suggested we go home and find the right documents and then come back for another appointment.

I got up and left. Leon followed me to the elevator and we rode down without saying a word to each other. Silent all the way to the car. Silent all the way to Chinatown. When I pulled up in front of the San Fran, he got out without a goodbye.

After school, I drove over to Salmon Alley for Leon's brick-colored suitcase—the one he arrived on Angel Island with—lugged the heavy thing down to my car, and went back to Mason's place.

I knew the story. One hundred and nine times I've heard Leon tell it. How buying the name Leong was like buying a black-market passport. How he memorized another man's history to pass the interrogation on Angel Island. And how later the government offered a deal: the confession program. How many of his friends went for it: Wong Min Fat, Jimmy Lowe, Lee Hoy. The exchange: a confession of illegal entry bought you naturalization papers. But Leon didn't trust the government; besides he never intended to stay. But fifty years later, here he was, caught in his own lie; the laws that excluded him now held him captive.

I lifted the suitcase up on to the kitchen table and opened it. The past came up: a moldy, water-damaged paper smell and a parchment texture. The letters were stacked by year and rubberbanded into decades. I only had to open the first few to know the story: "We Don't Want You."

A rejection from the army: unfit.

A job rejection: unskilled.

An apartment: unavailable.

My shoulders tightened and I thought about having a scotch. Leon had made up stories for us; so that we could laugh, so that we could understand the rejections.

The army wanted him but the war ended.

He had job skills and experience: welding, construction and electrical work, but no English.

The apartment was the right size but the wrong neighborhood.

Now, seeing the written reasons in a formal letter, the stories came back, without the humor, without hope. On paper Leon was not the hero.

Maybe Leon should have destroyed these papers. They held a truth about a Leon I wasn't sure I wanted to know. Why did he keep every single letter of rejection? Letters saying "We don't want you" were flat worthless to me. What use was knowing the jobs he didn't get, the opportunities he lost? I sorted through the musty papers, the tattered scraps of yellowed notes, the photos. I kept going; I told myself that the right answer, like the right birthdate, had to be written down somewhere.

Leon kept things because he believed time mattered. Old made good. These letters gained value the way old coins did; they counted the way money counted. All the letters addressed to Leon should prove to the people at the social security office that this country was his place, too. Leon had paid; Leon had earned his rights. American dollars. American time. These letters marked his time and they marked his endurance. Leon was a paper son.

And this paper son saved every single scrap of paper. I remember his telling me about a tradition of honoring paper, how the oldtimers believed all writing was sacred. All letters, newspapers, and documents were collected and then burned in a special temple, and the sacred ashes were discarded in a secret spot in the bay.

On Beckett Street once, Leon traced out the faint shadow where a paper receptacle had been attached to the wall. Another time, he pointed out an old man who had been a paper collector.

I made paper files, trying to organize the mess. Leon the family man. Airmail letters from China, aerograms from Mah to Leon at different ports, a newsprint picture of Ona graduating from the Chinese Center's nursery school, of Nina in her "boy" haircut and an awful one of me and Mason.

Leon the working man: in front of the laundry presser, the extractor; sharpening knives in the kitchen; making beds in the captain's room. Leon with the chief steward. Leon with girls in front of foreign monuments.

A scarf with a colored map of Italy. Spanish pesetas in an envelope. Old Chinese money. Dinner menus from the American President Lines. The Far East itinerary for Matson Lines. A well-used bilingual cookbook that I flipped through quickly: Yorkshire pudding, corned beef with cabbage, kidney pie. Had Leon been a houseboy?

Selections from newspapers. From *The Chinese Times:* a picture of Confucius, a Japanese soldier with his bayonet aimed at a Chinese woman, ration lines in Canton, gold lines in Shanghai. From *Life* magazine: Hitler, Charlie Chaplin, the atom bomb.

Leon, the business schemer: several signed and dated IOUs from You Thin Toy. Check stubs from Bethlehem Steel. A detailed diary of his overtime pay from Wa-jin Restaurant. Money-sent-back-to-China receipts. A pawn ticket from Cash-in-a-Flash on Fourth Street.

I felt my eyes crossing. Leon's goal had been to confuse the authorities but all he did was frustrate me. I told myself to concentrate and only look for that document I needed, the one with the right name and birthdate.

I went through another stack and something strange caught my eye: it was an affidavit of marriage.

In accordance with the marriage custom and practice long established, approved, and legally recognized in China; that no license or official recordation thereof at that time was required by the Chinese Government, and therefore no marriage certificate is now available; and that in lieu thereof, affiant executes these presents thereby and solemnly swears to the bona fides and validity of his marriage to the aforesaid. . . .

This wasn't even Leon's, what was he doing keeping other people's stuff? Looking closer, looking more carefully, I felt my shoulders pinch. It was Mah and my father's marriage certificate. I put it aside to deal with later.

Maybe the oldtimers had the right idea: keep everything and then burn it. That's what I felt like doing: gathering all Leon's papers, burning his secrets and maybe his answers, and then scattering the ashes into the bay.

I started throwing everything back into the suitcase, I took handfuls of papers up and pitched them back into the suitcase; I wanted to get everything out of sight. That's when I saw the photo of a young Leon, it was right there, Leon's affidavit of identification.

The photograph attached hereto and made a part hereof is a recent photographic likeness of the aforementioned Lai-on Leong, Date of Birth: November 21, 1924, Port of Entry: San

Francisco, is one and the same person as represented by the photograph attached to Certificate of Identity No. 52728 showing his status as a citizen of the United States.

It would do. I put the document aside and went back to collecting the rest of the scattered sheets. I packed everything—letters, official documents, pictures, and old newspaper clippings—back into the suitcase, and slammed the old thing shut. I thought, Leon was right to save everything. For a paper son, paper is blood.

Mason says I'm too much like Leon: I keep everything too, and inside I never let go. I remember everything.

Mason's right. I never forget. I'm the stepdaughter of a paper son and I've inherited this whole suitcase of lies. All of it is mine. All I have are those memories, and I want to remember them all.

SIX

LEON lost. Leon found.

I went looking for him at the usual places: the Universal, Woey Loy Goey, the Square. Finally Mason suggested calling Frank Jow. I hadn't thought of the Seaman's Union because Leon hadn't shipped in a long time. When I called, Frank told me that Leon had renewed his shipping card and paid extra to get onto the top of the standby list. Even Frank Jow was worried when Leon jumped at a job no one wanted: Watertender, Engine Department.

"Everything okay at home?" Frank wanted to know. "Everything okay with the family?"

Frank knew the answer to that. All of Chinatown knew. I was embarrassed about calling, embarrassed about lying. It was different when I was eight; I could say that Mah lost the itinerary or something. But this time, there was a desperate feel. I scribbled the information onto the back of a PeeChee folder: the arrival and departure dates, the ports.

Mason saw it coming. He said, "Disappearing is Leon's way of dealing. He needs time away." Mason wasn't worried the way I was; he figured Leon was safe. "On a ship, on a job, he'll be okay."

For forty days I'd held on, trying not to panic.

Now Leon was coming back and my plan was to pick him up and bring him home. Then Leon and Mah, Mason and me, we'd all sit down together for a meal. I was trying to make it like the old days, like those welcome-home parties Mah used to have for Leon. Mah was still mad about the way he left, but I'd made her promise not to bitch about it first thing.

The S.S. *Mariposa* was docking in Vallejo at nine, but Frank Jow said noon was probably the earliest they'd let the crew off. I wanted to meet the ship. Me and Mason showing up at the pier would surprise him, I was sure of that. I couldn't wait to see his face. Shocked and a little embarrassed was what I expected.

I had to take off half a day, which made it tense at work. Lynette Yee was upset because she was trying to work it so that I could slip into her position as the community-relations specialist, but I'd been taking too much time off. I couldn't help it, family stuff. Lynette was right, it didn't look good.

It meant losing a half day's pay for Mason too, but he offered to come with me. He knew I didn't want to drive all the way up to Vallejo and meet Leon by myself. I was grateful; Mason always knows when I need him without my having to say it all. I was supposed to be in front of the tunnel exactly at 11:30. Mason wanted to just swing by and pick me up. We're usually good about timing these things. But in the morning Edward Yee had cornered Denise Young in the closet and made her cry. There was a big scene and I had to take Edward to Principal Lagomarsino, who wanted me to get on the phone right away to translate to Edward's parents. I was pretty nervous, worrying about Mason circling around Chinatown during noontime traffic. If anything would piss him off, that was it.

And it happened. I missed him and he circled the congested streets twice, maybe three times; I didn't ask. And in an Audi he borrowed from the shop. Then we got on the freeway and traffic was slow going onto the Bay Bridge because an AC Transit bus ran into a Jaguar in the merge lane. Things were not looking good.

We inched past the accident. Mason glanced over and shook his head. "Goner."

I was telling Mason about Edward Yee, my long talk with Edward's mom, but Mason wasn't responding. It wasn't just the traffic that put Mason into a bad mood.

He said, "Jorge can't pay me this week again."

"That's three weeks." I flipped radio stations: news, KFOG, Jesus stuff. "You think he's doing drugs?"

"No. He's in over his head. He's buying too many dead cars. They just take up space."

There was nothing I felt like listening to, so I turned the radio off. I looked out over the gray rail, at grayer Oakland. We were sandwiched in between two trucks. Mason swung into the left lane. He continued, "He's after easy money. Buying and selling. I tell him to stick to fixing."

I knew Mason was thinking about getting out of Jorge's garage, but it's hard for me to know when I should say something. With Mason, I know better than to tell him what he already knows. Mason's one person in my life I don't have to worry about, to always think for. Mason can take care of himself.

PAST Richmond, we followed the signs to Vallejo, and as we rattled across the Benicia Bridge, I started remembering the route. You Thin had given me directions, just in case, but when I saw the moth-ball fleet on the bay, I recognized where I was. We got off the freeway and got on the main street and headed toward the pier.

At the corner, at a bus stop in front of a grocery store,

a group of men were kicking around. Restless. Leon was one of them. Mason made a quick U-turn, pulled right up. I buzzed my window down.

Leon looked shocked, then relieved, and even kind of happy to see us. He threw his bag into the backseat and said *adiós* to his friends.

"How you guys know?" Leon asked.

Mason said, "Frank Jow."

Leon nodded. Then he just looked out the window.

I watched the road, felt the car gaining speed, sliding back onto the freeway. I was feeling two things: I was glad Leon was back, but still angry. I really didn't care about his voyage, but I asked anyway. Habit, I guess.

"A lot of overtime," he said.

Mason said, "I've been doing a lot of overtime, too."

That interested Leon. "Oh, yeah? Good business?"

"Nah. I got my own side jobs going. My boss's been late with pay."

"Not good."

"No. Not good at all."

Leon leaned forward. "You set something up with your buddy. That buddy Zook. I help too."

I laughed. "Zeke."

Leon was quiet most of the way back down to San Francisco. He didn't seem to want to talk about this voyage. Maybe he felt he'd answered enough questions. I remember him coming home from voyages full of stories about the clean streets of Singapore, the beaches of Fiji, and the beggars on the Hong Kong waterfront.

After we paid the toll and were crossing the Bay Bridge, I turned and said to Leon, "Mah's cooking a real good dinner, your favorites."

Leon didn't say anything so I listed the dishes: "Bitter melon, Buddhist vegetables, bird's-nest soup."

Still nothing from Leon.

We took the Washington Street exit. Mason was veering right when Leon told us, "I'm not going to Salmon Alley."

I turned around and looked at him.

Leon's face was closed, shut off. He said, "You can take me to the San Fran."

"Mah bought the food already. She's home cooking it already."

Leon shook his head. "I paid up."

The car was going fast, but it didn't feel like we were moving at all. I asked Mason. "Now what?"

Mason glanced over his shoulder and said, "Leon, you want to go there now or later?"

"Now," Leon said.

Mason shrugged. "Guess that's what he wants."

I watched everything carefully as we drove up Washington. The streets were familiar, but I felt like a stranger. On Stockton, we stopped at a red light; an old woman dragged a little girl across the street. They passed so close I saw the child's crooked collar, her blue barrette.

At the San Fran, Leon got out. I didn't move until Mason said, "Take him upstairs, it's better."

Leon was already at the elevator when I caught up with him. We didn't say anything. Going up, we didn't look at each other. I followed him down the dark corridor to the end room by the fire escape. He had trouble with the key, and I was just going to help him when the lock turned. The door opened to the familiar musty odor of cigarettes and booze and tiger balm. I recognized the old-man odor. I looked around at the stripped cot, the rusty sink, the cracked windows, and I thought, all right. If this is where he wants to live, it's all right with me. I went back into the hallway and dragged his last bag in.

"Come and eat," I said. "You have to eat. We'll bring you back here later."

Leon looked tired. He shook his head. Forty days was a long voyage. "No," he said.

I just stood there, wanting to say: You're making this hard for me. But I said nothing.

"You don't know everything," he said.

"Tell me, then."

"Later."

I could barely hear him. I waited, looking at the deep cracks in the floorboards.

"Maybe later I tell you."

"Leon."

"Go." He shook his head. "She's waiting."

Mason knew that Mah hated wasting good food and suggested that we stop by and get Zeke to come for dinner. When I gave him a run-through on the events, Zeke tugged on his mustache and nodded, "Uh huh. I'm the buffer man, is that it?"

Mason smiled. "We're counting on you, man. Eat up. Make it look good."

"Can do."

THE apartment felt brighter, airier, lighter. There was a citrusy scent, of pomelo and the spritz of tangerine. Mah had arranged a pagoda stack of oranges, the plate like an offering, placed right on top of the television set. She had turned on every one of Leon's lamps.

Mason and Zeke hung back in the living room while I

went into the kitchen. Mah was standing over the stove, stirring soup.

"Zeke came, too," I said.

Mah smiled. "There's a lot of food."

Every burner was going. She turned the fire under the wok to high.

I just told her straight out. "We picked him up. But he wanted to go to the San Fran."

"He's there now?" A burst of color flushed her cheeks. She poured oil into the wok.

"Yeah." I watched the oil sizzle.

Mah sliced ginger from the root, whacked open garlic and threw the spices in. They popped, browning.

Mah made a throaty sound. "How'd he seem?"

"Okay. A little tired."

She threw the mustard greens into the smoking wok. I watched the green stems darken, the leafy ends wilt.

"Let him," she said. She yanked off her apron and threw it on the floor. "I don't care anymore."

She walked out of the kitchen, right through the bright living room down the corridor and into her room. The door shut with a bang.

I turned off the gas and scooped the vegetables into a platter and set it in the center of the table and brought out the dishes that were warming in the oven. I filled three bowls with soup.

Mason came in. "She okay?"

"No," I said. "She's pissed."

"Want me to ask her?"

I shrugged. "You could try."

Mason headed down the hallway toward her room; I heard him knock.

Zeke came into the kitchen. "Yeah, Mason and me, we could go in together, get a shop. We could make it work. What do you think, Lei?"

I turned away from him and rolled my eyes. Talking about cars again.

Mason came back shaking his head. "No answer."

I sat down; I picked up my chopsticks. "Let's eat."

Zeke picked up his bowl of soup; he slurped. "Hey, what's this soup again?"

"Bird's nest."

"Right, but I always forget, what's it made of?"

Mason grinned. "Bird spit."

Zeke drank up. "Sure is great stuff."

I filled three bowls with rice. Zeke flipped his chopsticks over the dishes, poked through the different layers of vegetables in the Buddhist dish. He nibbled on a stem of mustard green. "This is pretty Chinesey, huh?"

I HEARD IT. The rattle and groan of the old Singer.

Mah hadn't touched the machine in years. I thought I knew what she was doing. She was running the Singer, gunning the motor, letting the needle tear through an old strip of fabric until the thread ran out. Something I used to do after she and I fought. I'd go into the sewing room, turn on the Singer, take some old fabric out of the cloth bin and run it under the stamping needle. I'd just sew. The thread cone spun, the bobbin clicked. If I was mad enough, the hammering needle didn't scare me, I liked the danger: how the needle could nick the plate, break, fly upward. I'd let the needle fly until the anger ran out.

What was Mah feeling now? What did she regret?

Tommie Hom? My father? Leon? How did Ona weigh on her heart?

As Mason, Zeke, and I ate the dinner Mah made for Leon's return, I listened. There was something strange about the sound of the machine, a kind of echo behind the thumping. I listened hard and then I heard it clearly, a tinny hollowness: Mah was running the Singer without any fabric.

SEVEN

LEON showed up at Mason's shop one day and asked for a ride to the Chinese cemetery. Mason told me how he was under the Jaguar, almost finished with the job, when Jorge kick-tapped his shoe and said, "Hey, I think that's Lei's father out there." Mason couldn't figure why Leon was in the Mission, two bus transfers from Chinatown, and so he went out into the sun to see what was up. And there was Leon, hovering around the parking lot, peering into the windows of junked cars. The first thing Mason noticed about Leon was that wild look in his eye. I knew the look: that dead-fish glare that meant Leon was hooked on some scheme and didn't care about anything else. I was just glad Leon hadn't come looking for me at school.

"He didn't look good," Mason said, and he asked Jorge if he could take off early.

I thought about what a switch it must have been for Mason. One minute he's under a sleek machine, and the next he's driving around Colma with Leon, on some crazy cemetery search. And, of course, Leon got them lost. A half-dozen cemeteries and Mason kept asking Leon if he recognized any of them: Woodlawn, Pine Haven, The Holy Names, Green Lawn, Cumberland, Saint Joseph's.

But Leon kept shaking his head. "More dead than living," he said. "Where are all the Chinese buried?"

Mason circled the suburban streets until he saw a man walking a dog. He stopped and got all the way out of his car to ask directions. The old guy looked shocked to see

Mason, a long-haired Chinese guy in dirty overalls. But Mason had been driving around in circles, lost too long to care what anybody thought. All the cemeteries, all the streets, all the houses—everything—looked the same. The old man pointed up the street, but his voice sounded metallic, distant, like when Zeke called for a tool from under a car. Mason got the general idea: the cemetery for the Chinese was over the hill somewhere. Where? When the man repeated the directions, Mason saw the problem: the voice was coming out of a box attached to a hole in the man's throat.

Mason followed the directions until he came to a dead-end street. They could see the grass and stones and long shadows of the cemetery through a locked chainlink gate. Leon led Mason along the fence until he found a torn section large enough to crawl through. It was a messy-looking place, with overflowing garbage cans and half-singed funeral papers from Chinese burning rituals stuck in the bushes.

Leon led Mason along a path that rounded up toward a hill. He circled back down and around again. He scratched his head and stood there, moving his fingers, looking up at the sky. "He looked desperate," Mason said, "like he was trying to divine for the location."

Mason asked, "What's wrong? Where is it?"

But all Leon did was mumble something Mason couldn't quite catch.

When Mason looked at his watch, he couldn't believe it: near five, near closing, and there he was, standing on some cemetery hill, Leon beside him, muttering to Confucius or something.

Mason said he tried to help, but most of the names on

the gravestones were in Chinese. All Leon did was walk around shaking his head and saying, "No more, no more." Mason figured it was best to let Leon go at it on his own for a while. So he stood on the road and smoked a cigarette until he saw a security car cruising up the hill. He walked down to meet it because there was no telling what Leon might do in his obsessed state.

"Cemetery's closed," the guard said, as he got out of his car. A black man in a green uniform. "Cemetery's not open to the general public."

Mason told him that Leon wasn't the general public, that he was looking for his old man.

The guard shook his head. "Can't help you. This place is closed. You gotta come back. Monday Wednesday Friday. All day Saturday. And you gotta have a piece of paper saying you got people buried here."

"What kind of paper?" Mason wanted to know.

Just hearing Mason's tone made me nervous. Mason can't take that type of attitude, and it sounded to me like he was ready to throw one. There would have been a bad scene if Leon hadn't come up just about the time the guard said, "Hey! how'd you guys get in anyways?"

For once, Leon had the right interpretation of the situation, to help rather than harm. Leon's got the oldtimer's odd mix of fear and respect for a uniform, even a graveyard security guard's uniform. As a rule, I never trust how Leon sees things on the outside. He's better now. But what really annoyed me when I had to go around translating for him was that he had two faces: defensive or ingratiating.

That afternoon, luckily, Leon's deferential manner was just right. Leon got the guard off his asshole attitude by calling him Sir. He led the guard down to the fence and showed him the torn section. "Young fellas," Leon speculated. He held his hand in the air and squeezed fast, many times. He made cutting sounds. Then he crawled back out to show the guard how he'd gotten in when the cemetery was closed. Leon threw his head back and laughed.

Mason didn't like any of this: losing a half day's pay, driving around in a maze of suburban streets, getting directions from a man with a hole in his throat, sneaking into a graveyard in broad daylight, backing out on his hands and knees in front of some Mr. Procedure Guard. Leon laughing. The whole business pissed him off, he told me, The least Leon could do when he hit him up for a ride was to know where he was going.

I agreed. I sympathized.

Didn't help. Mason was still pissed. "Lei, you deal with it. Get the papers, follow the procedure. Find out where this grave is before Leon really loses it."

Mah wasn't surprised when I told her about Leon at the cemetery. "I knew something was cooking in that fry-pan head of his." She suggested going to the Hoy Sun Ning Yung Benevolent Association.

What to ask? Mah wrote everything down: Grandpa Leong's Chinese name (Leong Hai-koon) and his American name (Ah-Fook Leong), his village, his date of birth, and the date of his death. She handed me the information, remembering how nineteen years ago she'd written the same thing, but slipped that sheet into a glass jar to be buried in Grandpa Leong's coffin. "Insurance," the sewing ladies had advised. "In case of earthquake or war, people would know where the body belonged, where home was."

Mason thought I'd better go to the Benevolent Association alone. "No telling what you're going to find out, or how Leon's going to react. He can say a lot more stuff in Chinese."

Friday after school, I walked down to the five-story building at 41 Waverly Place. The narrow staircase squeaked. I stepped aside on the first landing to let some Italian guys carrying white carnation wreaths pass. On the second floor, the rumble of the machines and the odor of hot steamed linen made my nostrils feel prickly; these sensations brought back memories of working in Tommie Hom's sweatshop, helping Mah turn linen pockets. Ironing the interfacing for the culottes. The time I sewed my finger. The awful exactness of the puncture point where the needle broke nail and skin. An exacting pain.

A racket of mah-jongg sounds, plastic tiles slapping and the trilling laughter of winners filled the third floor. The fourth smelled of sweat. Sharp intakes of breath, sudden slaps, guys grunting. Master Choy, White Crane Gung-Fu Club.

The office of the Hoy Sun Ning Yung Benevolent Association was like many other Chinatown family-association offices: family and business mixed up. To the right, a long counter; to the left, the reception area, made up of two hand-me-down sofas, old arm touching old arm. More sofas behind the counter, their old backs touching. There were Boy Scout plaques on the wall, high school wrestling trophies on the end tables, and stacks of newspapers everywhere. A calendar on each wall and a government-green filing cabinet in each corner. The windows were dirty, the floral curtains a dusty blur. Xerox boxes were stacked dangerously high for this earthquake climate.

I stood at the counter for a while. There was a man or two on every couch, each one reading a newspaper. I couldn't figure the workers from the visitors. Finally, one man dropped his newspaper, noticed me, and shouted toward the back, *"Wey, a person's come!"*

A man came out from behind the screen. His face relaxed me and I just told him right off about Leon's going to the Chinese cemetery, looking for and not finding his father's grave. The man kept smiling a benevolent smile so I kept talking. I told him how upset Leon was, getting lost looking for the cemetery and then finding the cemetery but not being able to find the grave.

I shook my head. "It's shameful to lose a father's grave, even if it's not your real father."

"Not so shameful," the man said. "Maybe they move him."

"Move him?"

"Maybe," the man said.

"They move them?" This was news to me; I'd never heard of moving the dead around. "That's weird; are you sure?"

"Sometimes. Make more room. Always need more room. Every day." He asked for a receipt.

I said I didn't have a receipt but I showed him what Mah wrote.

The man looked at it and then disappeared behind the screen again. He came back with a manila file and handed me a page from *The Chinese Times.* "We ran this ad all of February." He told me overcrowding had become a problem at the cemetery and most oldtimers had only leased their burial plots for three, five, or nine years, hoping to be sent back to China by relatives. "More often than not," the man said, "the dead are forgotten. People get busy. Times change, even feelings. It happens."

He pulled out another sheet with columns of names that reminded me of the attendance registers used by my Chinese schoolmasters. I remembered standing at attention, waiting for my name to be read out loud. The schoolmasters chanted off our names so fast I was always afraid I wouldn't get my "Here, I'm here!" in before the next name was read.

Now, as I watched the man's long nail go down the three columns, I found myself holding my breath, afraid again. What if Grandpa Leong's name wasn't on this list of abandoned dead?

The man told me the list was published in all the other Chinese community newspapers: Sacramento, San Jose, and Los Angeles, and that the association waited through the Ghost Festival, which was close enough to the beginning of spring and the Easter holidays, for people to come in, for relatives to respond. Then they made the arrangements. That foggy summer in Colma, the unclaimed graves were disinterred and the bones grouped by family surnames and then reburied.

"There was a ceremony. Didn't you read about it? It was reported in the English newspapers." The man tapped the last name on the register with his yellowed nail. "Here he is, the last name."

I looked to where he was pointing and nodded.

"Sometimes it takes a generation, like you, but eventually somebody comes. Tomorrow, or another generation's tomorrow, it's all the same. Blood is blood."

I asked Leon's question. "How to get the bones back?"

"What?"

"The bones."

The man just shook his head. "Too late." He gathered

up all the newspaper clippings and papers, tapping the edges neatly back into the manila file.

"*Woh!*" A man sitting on a couch blew out his cheeks and shook his head. "That job would take a special kind of *gung-fu!*"

The association man agreed and pointed to the Xerox boxes and said, "All together, they're all in boxes that size." He handed me the permit I needed. I thought his voice deepened, became more fatherly. "Bow to the family head-stone, it's all the same, the right gesture will find your grandfather."

WHEN Grandpa Leong died, he left two things, a snake in a jar and a tame pigeon tied to his windowsill. The snake was soaking in a bottle of herbs, a medicinal wine; the pigeon had a lame leg. When we delivered his meals, Grandpa Leong liked to bring the pigeon inside and feed it the leftover rice. Grandpa Leong ate mainly vegetables, but once in a while he liked an oxtail stewed in medicinal herbs.

Grandpa Leong looked like the oldest of all the old men that we knew. He looked ancient, like one of the Eight Holy Immortals, a smart old god. We visited him when he worked on an alfalfa farm in Marysville, and there are pictures of all of us standing together in front of his wooden shack in the middle of the fields. He had a sun-leathered face, and so many wrinkles around his eyes that Ona called them elephant eyes. He didn't use a cane when he was on the farms. But when he moved too slowly for the work, he packed his stuff into a brown shopping bag, walked out onto the road, and flagged down a Greyhound bus heading south to San Francisco.

Leon was on a voyage and it was Mah who found Grandpa Leong dead. She never told what she saw, but when she was on the phone once, I overheard her say something about how it would have been better if he were lying down, in bed at least. Mah was upset about having to make all the decisions. She said she was willing to go along with making a decent gesture, but she didn't want to wear hemp and weep for a show. She said, "He's not a blood relation."

But Mah called Frank Jow at the Seaman's Union and found out that Osaka was the next port where we could get a telegram out to Leon. Mah and Ona and Nina and I took No. 15 Kearney to the Western Union office, where Mah wrote out the telegram. I still remember the address, even the voyage number: Leon Leong, American President Lines, Ltd., c/o S.S. *Independent*, Assistant Presser, Laundry Dept. V/103. We hoped Leon would be back in time for the funeral, but there was no guarantee.

Mah had a hard time handling everything. Grandpa Leong didn't have any savings, so she had to ask around for donations to pay for the casket and the burial clothes. She borrowed Tommie's van because the funeral house didn't have a hearse. She also asked Tommie if she could have a half day off and advance pay. Mah was his favorite seamstress at the time, so he didn't have a problem with it. He even offered to drive the coffin out to the cemetery. It was all the asking; Mah said she felt like she owed everyone; that was what humiliated her.

At the factory, Mah cried when she thought no one could see. The sewing ladies all seemed extra nice, giving their old-country advice, asking if they could help, but Mah always shook her head. At home, late at night, she would ask me: Should we have a wake, too? What kind of coffin? Should it be open or shut? What to write on the gravestone? How to pick a burial site? Was Nina too young to go? Should we all wear hemp? Who would sing the lament songs? Should we hire a professional mourner?

My bedroom was also the sewing room, so I lay in bed, listening to all Mah's worries. They kept coming, one by one and then repeating again. In between, the motor ran. I don't remember having much to say at all. All I remember is staring up at the ceiling, waiting for sleep, wishing for the right answer.

THE Saturday before the funeral, the Saturday we expected Leon to come home, Mah just broke down. I was at the shop, helping turn the corduroy pockets for the peacoats. She was worrying about whether or not Leon was going to get home in time.

"Hope so. Probably," I answered in an automatic tone.

Suddenly, Mah bolted up, her chair flipped back, and she was running toward the door. Tommie was just coming in and his arms were full of bulky bundles. Tommie must have seen something that made him drop everything. All I saw was Mah flying into his arms.

Production stopped, and everybody stared at Mah sobbing into Tommie's big chest. That was the first time I was in the shop when it got machineless quiet: not a motor rumble or a thread-spool roll, not even a steam press hiss. Only the Cantonese opera was still going, the cat voices screeching on, out of tune and out of context. (A love story about ill-fated cross-dressing lovers.) But the whole machine racket started up, suddenly, and louder than before.

Several ladies went and gathered Mah into their arms,

away from Tommie. I remember watching and thinking that maybe true comfort came only from the arms of other women. The sewing ladies' cooing voices did seem to ease Mah's sobbing. They shook her shoulders, urging her to listen: "Loosen your heart from the matter. He's not your father, he's not a blood relation. You're just doing what a good person should. Helping a poor man out, being a good person. Don't think too much. You'll get sick." They talked about fright as if it were a poison Mah swallowed and everyone offered their own secret remedies: medicinal snake gall, a temple offering, sleep. I made faces at all their suggestions, which brought attention to me. Luday looked over at me and said in a somber voice, "You have your girls."

Only Miss Tsai, who worked the machine directly across from Mah, hadn't gotten up. I thought she had a haughty attitude; she acted like she was so much better than everybody because she was from Hong Kong. All the ladies snickered about her bouffant hairdo, her high heels. Laughing, they said, "If she's so Hong Kong smart, what's she doing in a sweatshop?"

That day, Miss Tsai was the only one to stay seated in her metal chair; she didn't say a word till Mah sat down to work again. Then Miss Tsai said she understood Mah's behavior. "No one's blaming you, finding the old man dead, and like that."

I heard the "underneath thread" of her heart.

Mah heard too, I'm sure, but she never gave Miss Tsai the satisfaction.

Mah sewed. A straight seam roared on, nonstop. Scissors clicked, snipping off the end threads.

"Besides, with your husband away so much," Miss Tsai

said, looking up, sly-eyed, ". . . it must be hard. A woman alone."

I looked at Miss Tsai, I looked at her hard.

Mah didn't say anything, didn't even blink. Mah wasn't fooled by the false front of comfort. She sewed harder; the needle roared, the motor belt gunned.

Seeing Mah in Tommie Hom's arms, I knew there was more to it than just finding Grandpa Leong. It had to do with Leon being gone so much, it had to do with the monotony of her own life.

It wasn't just death that upset Mah, it was life, too.

IF Grandpa Leong had been a family man, he might have had real tears, a grieving wife draped in muslin, the fabric weaving around her like burnt skin. The wife might have wailed, chanting the lament songs. Other women, older aunts, might have had to support her at the elbows, ready to pull her back if she tried to throw herself on the coffin. Brothers and cousins and in-laws might have all come, everybody weak, everybody woeful. They would have argued about which was the luckiest burial plot. Facing east? Facing west! Over the years, they would have spied on each other—who visited the grave on the Ghost Festival? how much grave food was offered? how much paper money was burned? They would have counted each other's oranges. Hopefully—and there was hope if there were children—when his children were grown and making their own money, they'd dig up his bones, pack them in a clay pot, send them—no, accompany them—back to the home village for a proper burial.

The funeral house where Grandpa Leong was prepared

was as makeshift as his coffin. Its storefront windows faced Portsmouth Square, and the heavy sheets that were hung to shut out the light looked like old rubber mats they used on the floor of fish stores. There were a few quickly nailed-together benches, and in one corner, stacks of boxes with odd bits of bright, leafy debris. I remember that there was a certain coolness in the room, a lack of scent. Later, Leon told me this was the poor man's funeral house; it didn't even have a name; men with families went to Cathay House on Powell or to the Green Street Mortuary.

I learned later that the funeral parlor doubled as Shing Kee Grocery's warehouse, and that they only leased it out for funerals. The space went on to house other things: Everybody's Bookstore, Master Kung's Northern-style Martial Arts Club, and the Chinese Educational Services.

AT Grandpa Leong's funeral, Ona, Nina, and I sat on the front bench, watching an old woman tend the ritual burning by the coffin. The smoke hurt our eyes. Ona leaned over and whispered that Grandpa Leong's coffin looked cheap. I agreed that the splintery boards balanced on two stools made a wobbly-looking thing.

We watched the old men file slowly up to the coffin. Each old man approached the coffin alone, bowing to both ends of the box. The Newspaper Man from the Grant and Washington corner tucked something inside the coffin. The man from Grandview Theatre bowed from the waist like a movie star. I recognized a chess player, the herbalist, a butcher from Hop Sing's, a waiter from the Universal. They all went straight up to the coffin, bowed and then came to tell Mah they had to leave and go back to work.

When there were enough people seated, Cousin stood up and walked to the front of the coffin and gave a speech about Grandpa Leong's life. He told about how Grandpa Leong came first to mine gold and then settled into farm work around the Valley. He named all our names. He apologized for not having more to tell, but he said he only knew Grandpa Leong through Leon's stories. Nina squirmed; Ona swung her legs under the wooden bench; I gave them both a look that meant, Stop it! Mah hissed at us.

Mah, Nina, Ona, and I went up to Grandpa Leong and bowed our last goodbyes. I saw his powdery beard and his blue borrowed suit; I read the words HELL BANK NOTES on the fake money that was scattered across his chest.

We stood in front of the door and old men filed past; some touched our heads, most mumbled in Chinese. They nodded at Mah, who handed each of them red and white envelopes. We got them, too. We pocketed the red ones. Ona leaned over and whispered the amount to us. We knew the quarter was for buying candy to bring the sweetness back into our lives. We ripped open the white ones and threw the mourning paper immediately onto the ground in the deliberate gesture Mah had taught us the night before. (White is the mourning color, she said; throw it away from you.) The butterscotch Lifesaver had a cellophane wrapping that was colorless, but to be safe, I trashed it, too. I popped the Lifesaver into my mouth, not expecting to like it, but knowing I couldn't refuse the funeral candy. The Lifesaver took a long time to dissolve but when the rich, buttery taste filled my mouth, I felt better.

We walked outside into the alley and the sun hit hard, hurting so much I wanted to go back into the parlor.

Mah carried Nina. Ona clung to her other hand. I leaned my face into Mah's dress and smelled the scorchy trace of just-pressed linen. I recognized the smell because of all the interfacing I ironed (and burned) the season A-line linen shifts were popular. It's easy to burn linen because high heat and a heavy hand are needed to get the deep wrinkles out. I still love how linen breathes, how, after many washings, the weave softens, supple as skin.

But the day of Grandpa Leong's funeral, Mah's new linen dress scratched my cheeks, burned my nostrils, and made my eyes sting. All I could think of was the dozens of hotly ironed dresses hanging in Tommie's airless factory.

Cousin, Croney Kam, Jimmy Lowe, and the Newspaper Man had a hard time getting the large coffin out the narrow, angled doorway. It became a noisy affair. The men jostled the long box back and then pushed it forward, rocking it out. Then they argued about how to get the coffin onto the van. Jimmy Lowe climbed up onto the van and tugged. The men lifted and heaved, pushing and grunting, and then with a scrape and a bump the long box was in. Tommie Hom slapped the sawdust off his pants, jumped down, and slammed his doors shut.

A row of dark suits lined the alley. The old men stood with their canes hooked over their elbows, their hats in their hands. The van started up with a burst. One old man said, "Too sad. No trumpets."

Mah, Nina, Ona, and I made a small and slow and quiet procession behind the van. Ona and I threw the long strips of funeral papers into the air, then we turned back to see them littering the alley.

"Wave!" Mah said.

The van turned onto Sacramento Street and then picked up speed. We stood at the mouth of the alley watching it move toward the direction of the three big roads: the bay, the bridge, and the freeway. We waved until we couldn't see the boxy shape anymore.

When Leon came back, he took us to visit Grandpa Leong's grave during the Ghost Festival. We wore the matching pale pink linen dresses Mah made for the occasion. The cemetery was full—three generations in every cluster—grandparents and parents talking loud, kids playing chase games. It was more crowded than Portsmouth Square, and I had the odd feeling that this was like a school field trip—the hot sun, the wide sky, and especially the minty eucalyptus smell, all so different from Chinatown.

Mah stacked the oranges and laid out the grave food: a dried fish, a whole chicken, and some steamed sticky cakes. Leon started a fire in a large tin canister, slipping paper money into the weak flames. When the wind snatched the dollars up, we ran to catch back the half-singed hell notes. Leon posed us in front of Grandpa Leong's grave and took pictures with the new camera he'd bought in Japan. But he didn't know how to use it and we stood in the hot sun so long I felt like I was wearing a metal helmet. I squinted at Leon to hurry; Nina stamped her foot and started to cry.

We were disappointed when the pictures came back, a whole 36mm roll of film and only one picture came out. It was of Ona. She's standing alone in front of the wooden gravemarker, holding a big orange in her hand.

WE DIDN'T go back to the cemetery until that Saturday I took Leon. On the way there, Leon said he wanted to bring Grandpa Leong an offering, so I pulled over at OrangeLand and he bought a whole sack. The label read GOLD COINS.

Leon was quiet all the way there. I pulled up to the gate and parked; I showed the guard our pass. I followed the directions I got from the Benevolent Association and walked toward the eastern base of the hill. We passed an old-style tomb and I pointed at the large mound rising out of the earth like a pregnant belly: "That's why there's no room. Why don't they move that one?"

Leon, curious, couldn't resist going up to the tablet to see who it was. He came back laughing and told me, "Cousin used to fool around with his wife."

The clouds hung low. We walked against the wind, up the hill, and I started to feel a dull ache growing behind my eyes. We moved over the rain-softened earth following the directions I had until we found the gravestone for the Leong family.

"Leong" was carved in bold strokes and fit into a large moon shape. Below, in a squarer script, the many rows of personal names were lined up like an army.

Leon leaned the sack of oranges against the Leong stone. He tapped down three rows of names and pointed at the last one. "Long time, Grandpa Leong."

Leon read other names: Leong Bing, Leong Kok-min, Leong Tien-fook. Leon remembered them; they had lived at the San Fran too. "Good," he said. "All old friends." Leon took out a pack of Lucky Strikes from his pocket and put it under Grandpa Leong's name. The red box stood bright against the soil, and I remembered what the man at the Benevolent Association had said: "The right gesture finds."

Leon stood sadly, with both hands deep in his pockets. Hidden fists. A firm horse stance. What was he thinking? I knew he blamed himself. The misplaced grave, the forgotten bones. Leon gave those bones power, believed they were the bad luck that stirred Ona's destiny. There was no way to talk about it. This was Leon's thing, and I'd learned the only way to respect it was to leave it alone. I walked around, looking at the other family stones. I listened to the heavy hum of the freeway, the whoosh of wind. I could feel the wind coming in slow drifts up through the trees.

The pack of Lucky Strikes made sense to me; this was Leon's ritual. The cigarettes were breath. Like the funeral candy that called back sweetness, the cigarettes called back breath. Leon's gestures toward the grave became a part of his own private ritual. This wasn't all about Grandpa Leong. Leon was looking for a part of his own lost life, but more than that, he was looking for Ona.

Ona had always been the forward-looking one. She was always excited about the next day, the tomorrow. She wanted to grow very old, as old as Grandpa Leong; Ona wanted to be a smart old goddess. She wanted to be a seawoman and sail the world, to see everything Leon saw.

Ona was a counter. She counted the one hundred and forty times our pet rooster crowed in his short life; she tried to keep count of the number of culottes Mah sewed one summer (Mah sewed faster than Ona could keep count). She counted off the days till Leon was coming home, and then she stood at the mouth of the alley, counting the cabs that went by. Every night that Leon was gone, she'd count out ninety-nine kisses to keep him safe, to bring him back.

Ona was right about the counting. Remembering the

past gives power to the present. Memories do add up. Our memories can't bring Grandpa Leong or Ona back, but they count to keep them from becoming strangers.

Leon had it all turned around, what he said to Mason that first time they went out to the cemetery, about there being more dead than living. If Ona were here, she would count the living; Ona would tell us that there are more living than dead.

EIGHT

IN the months after Ona's death, Leon and Mah fought all the time, about everything, everywhere: on Salmon Alley, at the Baby Store, the bank, the butcher shop. They even fought about where to put Ona's ashes. Mah moved them from the mantle, where I'd put them for the service, to the sewing table, to the top of the television. I don't know what she was doing. It was like she was trying to find the right spot. But there wasn't a right spot. I could see Leon getting agitated. In the end, she asked him if she could put Ona's ashes on Confucius's altar. Leon didn't say anything. He just left.

There's that old saying about couples: they fight at one end of the marriage bed and make up at the other. But Mah and Leon were fighting at both ends and the middle. Leon wasn't even sleeping at home. The gossip ladies came to the Baby Store to tell Mah what their husbands reported to them. Leon was sleeping on the sofas of the family-association office, on the long bench at the chess club, on a cot in the basement music club on Waverly Place. Leon not sleeping with Mah wasn't new, and it didn't bother me when he slept at the old-men clubs, but then Tina Ho, a teacher's aide at school, told me about the night Leon came to her house to play chess with her father. She said she offered to drive him home, but he said he'd rather sleep in the armchair. That bothered me.

Mah had her way of getting under my skin, too. I could

deal with her grief over losing Ona, but I couldn't deal with her whining about Nina being in New York. I told her New York was far but it wasn't dead.

I had my own resentments. I resented Nina her fast move, her safe distance; I resented her three thousand miles. I resented Leon's madness, his blind lamenting to Confucius, his whole hocus-pocus view of the world. I resented Mah her stubborn one-track moaning—crying over Ona who was dead, crying over Nina who was gone. Crying over her two lost daughters. I wanted to shake her and ask, What about me? Don't I count? Don't I matter? There I was, the living present daughter, and Mah was hung up on the other two.

I wasn't dead. I wasn't gone.

Actually, I was glad Nina was gone. It was easier to talk to her long distance. I even looked forward to calling her on Sundays to complain about Mah and Leon. Taking Mah to Hong Kong was Nina's idea. She said a trip would do Mah good, a change of place does wonders.

"She won't go on her own," I said. "It's been over twenty-five years." I had the feeling Mah was afraid of going there alone.

"I have some vacation time, I'll take her."

That surprised me, Nina offering to do everything. She arranged it all in New York: the discounted ticket, a direct flight. She even sent Mah's ticket out Federal Express.

"Just get her on the right flight," she said. "I'll meet her there."

Mah wanted to keep the Baby Store open while she was gone but she wouldn't ask Leon, and I made it clear I didn't want to do it, so she asked Luday. When I helped Mah pack, I was glad to see her getting excited. She had some outdated ideas about presents, though. She wanted to take old clothes for the relatives. I told her old things might have been all right thirty years ago, but now people wanted everything new. Mah said something sweet would be good, so I bought her a couple of boxes of Mrs. See's candies. She made a big deal about buying a few pounds of an expensive brand of American ginseng.

I did what Nina asked and got Mah to the airport and made sure she got on the right flight. I felt good—good guilt—watching her walk through the gate. She turned back and waved.

"*Ho lo, ho lo*," I said. "Have fun, have a good trip."

GOING back, I sped. I knew Mason didn't like that I stayed with Mah and only visited him on weekends. Mason's a little like Leon, only instead of disappearing he just explodes. I could sense something coming on but I don't know what was wrong with me. I could see it coming, but I couldn't get motivated to move out on Mah.

I whipped along in the Karmann Ghia, through the slower-moving traffic, feeling pretty good, starting to feel relieved. Nina and Mah were out of sight for ten days, a fist of time. I gave the engine more gas and exited at Mission Boulevard.

I made one quick stop for a bottle of champagne. Walking into Mason's place felt like coming home. It felt like *I* was the one going on vacation.

After Mason opened the champagne, he brought out a stick of hash. At first I worried—Mason quit doing drugs last year. But I didn't want to get into a fight about it; besides, I wanted some myself. Mason winked and told me it was laced with opium, and after a few puffs, I felt even better, kind of buoyed up, lulled.

Mason's body is lean and tight and I love watching him. It still surprises me, how fast my body responds to his touch and how smoothly he moves me around, how I can almost read the heat in his palm, his palm on my back, a nudge of his knee, his knee pressing me down. The slow kiss at the small of my back and the toughness of his callus-knotted hand moving over my breasts, pinching. In the mirror he likes to keep by the bed I watched him smiling that slow, sly smile, wondering what he thought. I wanted to kiss those smooth shut lids. What? I wanted to know. He licked my ear and said something wild, then opened his eyes, looking at me in the mirror. I turned over and pulled him down, locking him in. We pushed and rocked, the sex pushing everything out of my head—all those weeks of family worry, all my fears about Mason's being mad at me for not being here.

It crossed my mind what Nina said, about how she liked a guy that could talk through sex. I told Mason. I said that my gut feeling was a guy who spent on talk was wasting. Mason laughed and said it shouldn't take too many words to get something right.

Then I started mumbling about how I appreciated that he hadn't bothered me about moving back during all the problems the last few months. "This trip'll relax Mah, you know, and maybe . . ."

"Don't worry." Mason stroked my head. "You worry too much."

We dozed and woke up starved. It was dark by the time we finished our burritos at the taqueria down the block. We stopped at the corner bodega for some groceries: juice and milk and bread for the morning, chips and beer for that night. Mason carried the large sack. I linked an arm around his, a gesture that made me think of an old photo I have of Mah and Leon, looking happy in love, walking along old Grant Avenue.

It was early and it felt good just hanging out. Mason went downstairs for a couple of hours to work on his car and I corrected papers. After the late news, he told me I better check on Leon. I said he probably wasn't even home.

Mason said, "You never know."

I laughed. "Maybe next week we can take him out to dinner."

"Maybe," Mason said.

I called Salmon Alley on the outside chance, on the *way* outside chance that he might be home. Leon answered on the first ring. "You be the eat already?" he asked.

I told him burritos and he laughed. "Too much beans."

"What are you doing home?"

There was a moment of quiet before Leon said, "Croney Kam say Mah go to Hong Kong."

"Nina took her," I said.

I thought maybe he didn't hear me, but in a minute he said, "That's good."

"Next time I'll take you."

Leon liked that idea. I asked him if he'd eaten, and he said not yet, he was working on something. "You come around, I show you."

"You're going to sleep at home?"

"Where else?" he said in Chinese, and I couldn't tell if he was being sarcastic. I started to get riled up. Did he think I didn't notice he was gone the last month? Did he think the sewing ladies had stopped talking all of a sudden?

But I didn't want to get into a bad mood at Mason's, so I just asked him if he wanted to go out for dinner next week.

"Any day," Leon said. "I be the home. You come by any day."

After I hung up, I was suspicious. "Leon sounded strange."

"How?"

"I don't know, he sounded happy. Maybe he's drinking."

"No," Mason said, "your Mah's just gone is all."

I was as relieved as Leon. Odd, but Mah's not being around helped; her absence lessened the weight somehow, as if she'd taken some of our sorrow about Ona far away.

Mason and I had a great binge week. I felt looser; it felt good to be with Mason full time. I never worry about Leon in the same way I do about Mah, he's used to being alone. Mason and I ate at the taqueria most nights or took out from the Vietnamese place on Twenty-fourth. Zeke and Diana came over Saturday and we made chile verde, got high, and then went to a club. We talked about going wine tasting the next day, but when Zeke called the next morning, we were too wiped out, and Mason told them to go on themselves. We slept late, then Mason took me for a drive in the Jag he was working on. We cruised down the Great Highway onto Highway 1 and stopped in Half Moon Bay for a late brunch at a cute place called The Gull. Mason talked about cutting back on hours at the garage and working up his freelance business. I knew he wasn't getting along with Jorge, so I said it was a good idea. I told him I was thinking about a change myself, that I'd liked the home visits I made with Lynette, that the liaison work felt natural, and if the community-relations position opened up, I might think about it.

I told him it was easy. "Going into the homes, talking to parents."

"Yeah," Mason said, "you've got experience."

WORK was crazy that week. We were getting ready for open house and Miss Schmidt wanted fresh bulletin boards. It was a big project—huge sheets of construction paper, rulers, and marking pens. I left all that stuff on the living-room floor so I wouldn't have to set up every evening. The clutter reminded me of Leon and all his oddball projects, how Mah used to bitch about his stuff being all over the kitchen table when she had to cook, so I checked to see if it bothered Mason, but he said he didn't even notice it.

Friday night, I called to remind Leon about dinner. He promised to be ready and waiting outside the alley at six, so Mason and I swung by, looking for him to be leaning against the wall in his double-breasted gangster suit. But he wasn't there.

Before I even got inside the apartment I could smell the junkyard odors: old oil and grease and rusting metal. And what I could see in the half dark was worse than what I smelled. I stepped over the piles of junk, old toasters and radio parts, old antennas—dumpster quality, all of it. Something crunched underfoot but I moved on, not caring what I destroyed. The living room was an even bigger junkyard. There was a bare bulb hanging over an old coat rack. In that strange factory light, everything looked dirty and grimy and completely useless. It was a disaster area. Screws and wires and lampshades, the shells of clocks, a bowling ball. But in the middle of all of it was Leon in his American President Lines coveralls, holding a wire coat hanger over a flaming torch. I shouted out my hello but stood back, not trusting whatever it was Leon was fixing. It looked to me like something was going to blow up.

Mason went up to him and said something. Leon looked up, said, "You know?" Then he threw his head back and laughed.

I saw the large black metal Singer machine on the floor by Leon's feet. It was all taken apart. On its side like that, it looked like the head of a horse.

"What'd you do to the sewing machine?" I was surprised at my accusing tone. Mah hardly used the thing anymore, but I remembered all the party dresses she'd sewn, all the culottes I'd helped sew. I liked remembering those nights, and I didn't like seeing Mah's machine in pieces all over the floor.

Leon looked at me. "Broken. I fix him for Mah. Be the surprise."

Smiling, he just stood there, in the middle of all his junk. His patch pockets were sinking, tool-heavy to his knees. I looked down at his feet and thought, what was he doing, wearing rubber thongs with all that jagged metal stuff around? Why didn't he wear those army boots with the steel-enforced toes he liked so much?

I didn't want to get into a fight, so I walked back down the hall to my room, sat down on my bed, and waited. Mason would take care of it. I heard more talk, then laughing and louder talking, and then Mason came to tell me that Leon was changing clothes, getting ready. He sat down and put his arms around me and shook my shoulders and said, "Hey, stop it."

"The machine's a wreck," I said.

"He's fixing it."

"No one's touched it for years!"

"He's got a week. Let him have his space."

I sure wasn't going to clean up after him this time. I gave Mason a look and said, "I hope you're good with sewing machines."

MASON borrowed a Mercedes from work to pick up Mah and Nina. "Nina's going to love this," I said on the way there. "Leon looked disappointed we didn't ask him."

"I'll take him for a ride before I deliver the car. Maybe tomorrow."

"No, I mean to pick Mah and Nina up."

Mason shrugged. "He'll see them soon enough."

"Can you believe he actually put that machine back together?"

I felt the car going, picking up speed, jetting onto the freeway. "Yeah," Mason said. "I can believe it."

Mah looked great, a good ten years younger. She'd finally put on some weight, and her coloring came back, a glow. She wore her makeup like she did in the old days, her Tommie Hom look, matchstick eyebrows and high-tone rouge and red lipstick. Mason told her she looked good and she beamed, kissing him, patting his arm.

Nina was wild about the Mercedes. She slid into the front seat and said, "Whose is it?"

Mason said, "Want to go on a blind date?"

"Cute?"

"Let's say he could work out."

Nina said, "No thanks. I'm through with guys that need a lot of work."

"Frog bodies," I said.

Nina bounced in her seat. "Hey, but, Mah, didn't I meet a prince in Hong Kong?"

I looked over at Mah. "Really?"

Mah squinched her nose and said in a joking tone, "Playboy."

"You got some pictures?"

"He Chinese?" Mason asked.

"Course!" Nina said, sounding a touch defensive. She went on, making a case for him by talking up his business: a travel agency. She was thinking about giving tour guiding a try. There were special shopping tours she could lead through Hong Kong and Europe. He thought she'd be good at it. "Kai says I'm a natural."

"Born shopper," Mason said.

"Kai?" I asked. "That's his name?"

"Yeah." That defensive tone again.

"Sounds Chinese," Mason said.

In Chinese, Mah asked about Leon.

"Great," I said in English. I told her he was actually in a real good mood, that he stayed on Salmon Alley, that we went out to dinner and he didn't make trouble with the waiters. "He even wore his gangster suit."

Mah showed me the new watch she'd bought for him. A fancy, black-faced, many-dialed diver's watch.

"Great," I said, "that's the kind he likes."

"This one works," Mah said.

MAYBE Mason was right, I worried too much. Not only did Leon fix the Singer, he polished it. And he pointed one of his lamps at the dark body so that it looked sinister in a bright shining way. The old floors looked scrubbed and the kitchen and bathroom were so Clorox clean they smelled like the YMCA pool. Leon was clean too, freshly shaved. He was wearing self-ironed dress slacks for the occasion.

I kept an interested eye on Mah and Leon. No formal hello, they just kind of bumped into each other. Leon looked a little shy, Mah, a little scared.

"Ho lo?" Leon mumbled. "A good trip, fun travel?"

Mah nodded. *"Ho ho."* Then she started on a long gossip ritual about the relations. "Blind Second Uncle's terrible fourth son gambled away his father's business."

"What kind of business?" Leon was interested.

"Who's Blind Second Uncle?" I wanted to know.

Mah answered, "Two cement trucks."

"Hor sick!" Leon moaned. "Cement's good business."

"All gone now," Mah said. "His wife's gone too. Ran off."

"The son's?"

"No, the father's, you remember her, she was there the time you went to Hong Kong."

"Yeah, yeah. Strange eyes. That one?"

I couldn't follow all this Hong Kong talk, so I went into the living room. It didn't matter who these people were, Mah and Leon seemed to enjoy talking about their problems almost as if realizing that other people had problems cheered them up. Strange medicine.

Nina's voice came, a bird tone from the other end of the apartment. I could tell she was giving Leon something just by her tone. It was her I've-got-a-present-for-you voice. She's given me a lot, too, and I admit I had a problem, feeling embarrassed because I was older and making less money. Nina's always been generous about her money, it's her time that she's a hog about.

Mason's voice: "Nice shirt, Nina. Got one for me?"

I heard them, their laughter swelling, their laughter making me think, I should get up and go out there. Resist and insist. I imagined Leon pushing the shirt back to Nina and Nina pushing it back to him. Back and forth until the shirt was completely unfolded. I've seen this ritual a thousand times. A part of me wanted to go and join in on the laughing, but another part just couldn't move. It was cozy in Leon's fat-man chair. I'd enjoyed the last two weeks not worrying about Mah or Leon. (To use Mah's favorite phrase, all I cared about was my rice bowl.) For ten days, I had been worlds away from Salmon Alley. With Mason, I could forget about all the problems. It freed me, knowing that Leon was lost in his projects and not likely to get in trouble and that Nina was taking care of Mah halfway around the world.

What I wanted was to hold everything still. Soon, I knew, the sorrow about Ona's death would come on like jet lag.

But I kept thinking ahead. Nina was leaving on the red-eye flight, to go back to her own life in New York. And how long would Leon stick around? I knew he'd leave sooner or later, and then what would I do? Move back in with Mah? What would Mason say?

I didn't budge, even when I heard Nina call my name again. That voice, the little-sister tone of it, made me freeze. That's when I saw the urn. Ona's ashes. The brass urn sat on the card table next to the sewing machine. I got up and walked over to it. Leon had made a whole little altar: a teacup with grains of rice, a teacup full of water.

After Mah left, Leon suddenly stopped talking about Ona. I thought he'd been happy the last ten days because Mah hadn't been around reminding him of Ona all the time. I thought he'd forgotten about Ona for a while, I thought that was why he looked so happy, he was drunk with forgetfulness. I thought I'd forgotten: with Mason. Nina thought she'd forgotten, with her new guy. Mah wanted to forget, with her gold mine of gossip. But nobody'd forgotten about Ona.

And here was proof: Leon's altar. He'd found a way to live with his grief. I could hear him say, Side by side, the sad with the happy.

I heard my name. I turned. It was Mason.

"Come on," he said. "Nina's got you a present."

NINE

THE news about Ona ran through Chinatown like a wild dog. Leon let it loose. When someone knocked at the door, he opened it. When the phone rang, Leon answered. He didn't care what other people asked; all he wanted to talk about was how much he loved Ona.

Leon was looking for someone to blame. All his old bosses. Every coworker that betrayed him. He blamed the whole maritime industry for keeping him out at sea for half his life. Finally he blamed all of America for making big promises and breaking every one. Where was the good job he'd heard about as a young man? Where was the successful business? He'd kept his end of the bargain: he'd worked hard. Two jobs, three. Day and night. Overtime. Assistant laundry presser. Prep cook. Busboy. Waiter. Porter. But where was his happiness? "America," he ranted, "this lie of a country!"

Leon always brought up the Ong & Leong laundry, but Mah didn't want to talk about how their business deal with Luciano and Rosa Ong went bad; she just wanted to forget. Mah went pale with shame just thinking about it. Not Leon. Leon talked about it to anyone who asked. He told the long and embarrassing story again and again. Mah didn't understand how he could face people; how could he walk down the street? She wanted him to have a thick skin, but it was like he was walking around Chinatown with no skin at all.

I thought he was on speed. He couldn't sit still. He went

spinning around the house picking fights with Mah, with me, even Mason. He flew around Chinatown trying to collect every debt owed to him. He wanted somebody to pay him back for all his suffering. His old cronies started to avoid him. Even Mason stayed in the Mission as much as he could.

What could we say? What could we do? Leon took any kind of reaction—a blink, a sigh, a glance—as an invitation to go on ranting. I tried to look as bored as I could, hoping that he'd eventually get tired and leave.

"Good! Go!" Mah shouted at his departing shadow. "I don't care what you say."

But it wasn't only the slam of the front door that lingered behind. Everything Leon said settled into Mah's mind. One time, Leon spit out Tommie Hom's name and Mah snapped right back, "And you? Are you so good? And you've never done wrong?"

So it went.

Blood and bones. The oldtimers believed that the blood came from the mother and the bones from the father. Ona was part Leon and part Mah, but neither of them could believe that Ona's unhappiness was all her own.

Mah blamed herself for what happened. She locked herself in her bedroom and pulled the curtains closed, shutting out all light. I couldn't get her to eat, much less talk.

Then the sewing ladies came and saved us. Luday, Soon-ping, and Miss Tsai came over on their afternoon break, still wearing their floral aprons. The three of them pushed in with their hello smiles, their arms full of food. Colored threads trailed in under their slippered feet. They brought wedges of sponge cake and special dumplings and a *boo* soup. They walked into Mah's dark room and passed it all under her nose.

Miss Tsai announced, "We only have fifteen minutes." Tommie had everyone working overtime; he had to deliver the linen dresses before the new year.

Luday passed me the food and started in with her bossy orders: "Put it into the refrigerator. Heat it up for your Mah tonight. Be a comfort."

I took the food from the ladies and went down the hall into the kitchen, but I moved slowly, listening. I knew they'd brought more than food for Mah; they'd brought their village advice. I heard Luday use Mah's personal name, and the intimate sound of it made me think about Mah as a young girl. Before Leon. Even before my father. I remembered other times I'd heard them call Mah by that name: when she found Grandpa Leong dead in his room, when Leon moved out after finding out about Tommie Hom.

Hearing her personal name must have soothed Mah. She nodded, listening as they told her what she had to do. They knew all the necessary rituals to get through this hard time.

I considered the odd course of our affinity: how often the sewing ladies were a gossiping pain and equally how often they were a comfort. Bringing the right foods was as delicate as saying the right words. The sewing ladies knew, in ways I was still watching and learning from, how to draw out Mah's sadness and then take it away.

Completion. Luday kept saying the word, as if repetition was a way of plucking the pain out. "Completion. Completely. All of it."

I don't know how to explain the effect the word had on me. Something about the way Luday said it was calming, her mouth rounding to mean "full," her lips meeting in a thin line to mean "still."

That was completion: change.

Soon-ping said, "Finish one thing before starting another." She meant, Finish your grieving before beginning the New Year.

But Ona jumped too close to the New Year. She made it hard for us. It sounds harsh in English, almost as if I'm saying she did it on purpose, that she wanted to make trouble. But that's not what I mean. All I wanted was to "finish one thing." When Soon-ping said it in Chinese, the phrase sounded true and soothing. Here was the New Year, an important time of celebration and beginning. And here was this sadness, this ending. Everything rushed ahead and then slowed to a swirl, a shoal of time around the New Year. These three days felt like forever.

I keep imagining Ona climbing up onto the ledge. Her legs pushing off, her arms flying through the air. Ona was falling and falling.

I want to open my arms wide as a fireman's net; I want to sweep over her whole life and comb out all the sadness that made her do it. Like Leon and Mah, I went over every moment I had with Ona and tried to find my own moment of failure.

Fault. In English or in Cantonese, that was the word we were all afraid of. I held it like a seed in my mouth. As kids, the three of us loved to suck on dried plums. Long after the sour and salty fruit dissolved, the seed stayed sweet, the true secret. Now I was afraid my secret guilt would start to grow sweet, and I would never want to spit it out.

The sewing ladies believed in village medicine; poison can draw out poison. Everything they said had a double effect. Mah cried, but the crying seemed to give her strength. She wanted to see the sewing ladies out, but they patted her hand and said, "No, no. Sleep now."

I walked them outside, where their voices turned grave.

"Terrible timing."

"And the New Year, only days ahead."

"Too soon."

Then they were quiet. Despite their comforting phrases for Mah, they were worried about attending a funeral so close to the festive days, afraid that death might follow them into the New Year. I told them not to worry, I'd made all the arrangements with the crematorium.

They turned away, looking down the alley, up at the sky, as if just hearing the word might be contagious. Their abrupt quiet made me nervous. I had to say something, so I gave them simple explanations I thought they could understand: the body was very broken; funerals were expensive.

They started to leave. I stood at the top of the stairs, watching them go down the steps. Miss Tsai tapped her watch and said, "Tommie."

NEW YEAR was Ona's holiday. She and Leon had a ritual; they laid out a feast for the gods: wine and fruit, a chicken, a fish, some steamed wheat buns. They lit the incense to call the gods down. The Eight Holy Immortals one year; the next, the Goddess of Mercy; another, it was the God of War paired with the God of Books. One year it was Jesus. Our Chinese School, Cumberland Presbyterian, handed out framed pictures of Jesus, and Ona believed him a god, too. And when Mao's Red Guards destroyed Confucius's temple, Leon invited the Great Teacher to come live with us.

This year, we didn't open the New Year, we didn't welcome any gods.

But Nina came home and I never felt so grateful for her company. We both took the sewing ladies' advice literally.

Finish one thing before beginning another.

To avoid thinking about Ona, we threw ourselves into housework. We had a cleaning frenzy. I swept and mopped and waxed. Nina did laundry and wiped down all the venetian blinds with soap and water. She dusted. I cleaned the oven, even the broiler we never used; I unscrewed all the gas knobs and scraped off the grime with a toothpick. Nina defrosted the refrigerator, a job I hated, and I scrubbed down the bathroom, one she hated. We re-stocked the kitchen with supplies to last till summertime.

NINA and I went together to return Ona's dresses to The Traders. We drove over the Bay Bridge to Emeryville. The manager, Eddie Jow, was so nervous he kept opening and closing his desk drawers. He stood up and walked around his small office like he was looking for a place to hide. He finally stopped fidgeting around long enough to hand me two jars: five spice and mustard seed. I slipped them into my bag. (They sat on Mason's kitchen counter for months, unopened, until finally I found the nerve to throw them out.) Eddie thought he was probably the last person to see Ona. He remembered nothing out of the ordinary that last night. After Ona paid out the tips to the waiters, she brought the charge slips and receipts and tally sheets with the cash bank into his office. Nothing strange. Ona's bank balanced, like always.

"She was one of my best hostesses ever," he said. "She had a fast mind. It was like she didn't have to think. She was always one step ahead of everybody. I told her, Stay in school. I told her, You're too smart to marry one of these waiters. Don't be fooled by a gold Rolex. All they got is a wad of tips in their pockets and alligator shoes on their feet."

That night was payday, so Ona stayed a while waiting for Eddie to find her envelope. "All I remember is, I gave her her pay and I said, See you tomorrow, like every other night I tell everybody, See you tomorrow, and she said, No, tomorrow I'm off, so I said, Yeah, okay, enjoy, have a good day off, something like that, and she thanked me and I said goodnight, get home safe, and that was it, she was gone. She looked tired. I remember a little tiredness around her eyes. And she was carrying her high heels in her hand. Walking around with no shoes on. But if you ask me, that's all I remember. A little tired. So what else is new at two in the morning?"

We hadn't asked him. That's the thing: people thought we wanted to hear about Ona, but mostly we just wanted them to be quiet about her. Nina wanted to get out of there, I could tell. It was almost four and the evening staff was starting to come in. Eddie told us he hadn't found a replacement yet, and I wondered if he was hinting that one of us might want to work the shift, take the job even, but I didn't say anything. Nina looked restless. I could tell what she was thinking. How could Ona stand a place like Traders, with all its fake Polynesian decor? All that bamboo and dried grass and fishing nets and red lighting. A barbecue chef in a glass cage that was made up to look like a thatched hut. Shrunken heads in a display case!

A chesty blonde came up to us and said she'd show us

where Ona's things were. She wore one of the pink dresses we were returning. As we followed the swooshing flowery print through the double doors, Nina whispered to me that it was even uglier on. In the bright kitchen, all the Chinese cooks stared at us. They spoke our dialect.

Them.

Sisters.

Look very like.

The dressing room was a linen closet. The hostess pointed to a pile of Ona's things: an old sweater, a pair of sneakers, a hairbrush, and a makeup bag. Nina slipped the hostess dresses out of her sack and then scooped up all Ona's stuff. She barely looked at it.

We were almost out the door when the hostess asked, "Are your parents really that strict?"

Strict? What did she mean?

I was strict with the kids at school. Chinese School was more strict than English School. We got whacked with a yardstick if our lessons weren't memorized. We paid a penny for every forbidden English word we spoke. That was strict. Absolute rules. Absolute punishments. To me, strict implies rules and order and consistency, some sort of agreement.

Mah and Leon had no such thing. They made up rules as they needed them, and changed them all on a whim. Mah had her ways when Leon was out at sea, but when he came home all her rules relaxed. Nina called their parenting chop suey, a little of everything. There were nights we had to speak Chinese at the dinner table and there were other nights we could laugh and talk English all we wanted and even take our bowls out to the front room and eat while watching *I Love Lucy.* One day we could run wild in the alley until way after dark and stay up all night eating candy and watching television. The next day we had to sew culottes until our eyes crossed.

The hostess said Ona used to talk about her and Osvaldo, all their problems.

Neither Nina nor I wanted to talk about Ona. I figured, Let her think what she wants, I'll never see her again.

But that wasn't all of it. Outside, the valet-parking attendant was waiting for us. He was a beefy white guy with a mustache. He followed us to our car.

"I'm really sorry," he said.

Nina nodded.

"I'm Matt. Matt Xavier."

I'd never heard of the guy.

"I drove her home," he said. "That night. And she seemed all right, the same. I mean, I drove her home a lot after Osvaldo stopped coming. And that night she seemed the same as always."

"Yeah," Nina said.

"She fell asleep on the bridge. She did that, fell asleep going over the bridge. She woke up on Washington Street, by the cable-car crossing, you know."

I was in my car. He had his hand on the door and he leaned in toward me and said, "I dropped her off in front of the alley."

I didn't want to hear about the last time he saw Ona. "See you," I said and pulled my door shut and put the car in gear and gunned out of the parking lot. I drove as fast as Mason out of the parking lot and then onto the freeway.

At the toll booth, Nina said, "Why does everybody keep saying she was all right?"

I shrugged, "Maybe they think they should've seen something."

Nina shook her head. "Ona could keep a secret better than anybody."

I said, "We're all pretty good at it."

We learned it from Mah and Leon. They were always saying, Don't tell this and don't tell that. Mah was afraid of what people inside Chinatown were saying and Leon was paranoid about everything outside Chinatown. We graduated from keeping their secrets to keeping our own.

But Ona kept more inside than either of us. I didn't blame her. Ona never had a chance with Osvaldo. Their getting together was too tied up with the Ong & Leong laundry. Leon's whole life was riding on the laundry, so when things went sour, Leon got dangerously old-world about his control over Ona. But she sneaked around with Osvaldo for a while longer before they broke up. Did they hold on to each other longer as an act of defiance? To try and prove Mah and Leon and Rosa and Luciano wrong? Who knows? All I know is that in that time Ona got used to keeping everything inside, to holding the seeds of herself secret from us, and we got used to her shadowy presence. Maybe being in the middle, Ona felt more stuck than either Nina or me. I think Ona wanted to be equally divided about her loyalties to Mah and Leon. But in the end Ona felt disappointed by Leon and betrayed by Mah. Why hadn't Leon seen his selfishness? Why hadn't Mah come to Ona's defense?

In my case, Mah and Leon's dependence on me gave me an uncomfortable power, too much control.

Nina said she watched us. She saw how I was locked into living Mah's and Leon's lives for them. She saw how Ona's need for them destroyed her. Nina said she always felt that by the time it got to be her turn, Mah and Leon acted like they'd given up on the family. So Nina decided to do things on her own. It didn't surprise me that she was the first to leave or that she went so far away. And there was nothing unusual about the fact that Nina had a new guy Mah and Leon didn't even know about. Still, I sensed there was a deep-down loneliness in Nina.

Rush hour, and we were stuck in the middle of it: the late-afternoon glare, the heat, the thick gasoline smell of idling motors, the tension of everyone wanting to be anywhere else but on that bridge.

"Maybe I'll tell them," Nina said.

"What?"

"About Michael."

That was the first time she'd used his name since coming home.

"Wait a while."

Nina was quiet for a while and then she said, "You're always thinking about them."

I was thinking that she only thought of herself, but I didn't say that. I said, "They don't need to know. What good would it do? This is the worst time."

Nina said no time was going to be good. "It's important to me; I want all this lying to stop. What do you want me to do? Call them and tell over the telephone?"

WE HAD some people over, close friends of Ona's, the sewing ladies, some oldtimers; just an afternoon when everyone remembered Ona before the old year ended.

ON SALMON Alley you can hear the New Year coming days in advance. At dusk, a scattering of firecrackers blasts through the streets. Around midnight, rockets flash into the sky like lightning. Every night the racket lasts longer until the carnival rises in Portsmouth Square and the dragon dancers wind down Grant Avenue, the streets turn red with spent firecrackers, and the air smells like lead.

We tried to put our grief away for the holiday, for good luck. Luday brought us a New Year fruit, a big pomelo. Miss Tsai brought a box of Mrs. See's coffee candy. Duckie's Mom came over and did Mah's hair for free, and Leon got a New Year's haircut so short it left a wide pale band around his ears. He wore his double-breasted suit. Mason bought me a fat gold heart on a chain. I gave him a manicure. Nina was already back in New York, and she called early so she could be the first to say Gung Hay Fat Choy.

Late afternoon, Mason came and took us all for a ride. He drove over the Golden Gate Bridge because he knew Mah loved how the light bounced off the cables, copper and bright gold, and Leon liked to remember the first time he sailed into San Francisco, how when his ship passed under the Golden Gate, the light disappeared for a long moment.

Mason suggested eating out, something we've never done on New Year. I caught a glimpse of Mah and Leon eyeing each other, conferring. Mason glanced at them in the rearview mirror. He said, "New Year, you're not supposed to cook, right?"

Mah gave me a vacant look. She does a quirky thing with her voice when she wants to say yes but is afraid to. "Oh," she said, "it doesn't matter. Whatever you want."

What got to me was the "oh." The sad and tired and put-upon tone, as if she wanted us to beg her.

Leon leaned forward between the front bucket seats, and said, "What? Where are we going?"

I said there was a new seafood restaurant called Ondine's, just over the bridge in Sausalito. Eating outside

Chinatown turned out to be a great idea. We all needed a change of scenery. Mah hadn't had much of an appetite, but she managed most of her swordfish. Leon didn't scowl at the waiters for not serving him with the same formality he lavished on the passengers on the American President Lines. I worried about the bill all through the meal, but when it came, Mason whipped it up, pulled a thick wad of cash out of his front jeans pocket, and counted out the twenties like a bank teller.

Early the next morning, we all left the house. Mah opened the Baby Store and Leon wandered down to Portsmouth Square to talk to the carnival workers. I went back to work. I walked through Alfredo's lot onto Mason Street and then down Broadway to Powell. I said good morning to Chuck Lee, who was setting out his vegetables. I waved to the noodle maker next door, and just like every other school morning, he raised a floured hand back. On Stockton, the butchers at Hop Sing's ran from the truck into the store, flesh-pink pigs thrown across their shoulders. A man in a short-sleeved shirt carried a stack of bread trays. Live fish poured from a rust-colored truck into huge plastic containers while men in rubber aprons watched, squinting over their cigarettes.

Everything seemed strangely new, as if I'd been gone so long I'd forgotten the relief in hearing those small sounds: splashing fish, a tray sliding out of its rack, and the easy chatter of the workers before the business day began.

At school, my message box was crammed with cards and notes from the teachers and staff. But they left me alone. No one hovered around sad-eyed and sympathetic, which I appreciated. Kevin Lum sent a Hallmark card, and I found phone messages from Mimi Fong and Belle Char. I didn't recognize the handwriting on one card, so I opened it. It was Serena from Galileo High. She said she wanted to talk, she needed to talk. Would I please call her? She signed it "Sincerely." Something about her handwriting I didn't like: the curls and loops and tiny circular "i" dots. The note looked like something out of a yearbook. I knew most of Ona's high school friends, but I had no mental picture of her. I wondered if this was the same Seri whom Ona called a back stabber, a two-faced liar. I slipped the card into my bag. Let her wait, I thought. I wasn't so sure about her sincerity.

The first thing I saw when I walked into the classroom was the paper dragon floating across the entire back wall. It shimmered, red and gold. The kids had filled the outline I'd drawn with at least a hundred scales, each one sparkling with glitter. I told the class that they'd made a beautiful New Year dragon, and they seemed happy, but they were uncharacteristically quiet all morning. They knew about my sister. They'd seen Miss Lagomarsino's face at the classroom door. They'd watched me walk out of the room in the middle of the morning and not come back. They'd heard their parents talking.

It felt good to be sitting at the back of the room in my wooden chair. The kids asked me simple questions about math and spelling and I was grateful to have the answers.

But it didn't last. After school, Serena Choi was waiting for me outside the gate. She came right up to me and told me she wanted to talk. I didn't recognize her at all. Her handwriting had given me the wrong impression: Serena wore her bleached hair short like a boy. She wore heavy eyeliner, tight Levi's, and a leather motorcycle jacket. She wanted me to go have a coffee with her at Caffe Trieste.

"Talk," I told her. I dropped my book bag and waited. I planted myself at the base of the steps; I wasn't going anywhere with her. My hardness surprised me.

I listened to Serena's confession right there on the front steps. In high school, she'd masterminded a whole year of harassing Ona. Late-night phone calls, hate mail.

"You beat her up that time," I said.

Serena looked away. "I still feel bad about that."

"It was a long time ago," I said. "Forget about it."

"I always wanted to say I was sorry."

I saw my chance and I took it. "It's too late now."

Serena looked about ready to burst into tears. But I didn't care if I hurt her. Let her cry. Why should I spare her feelings? If she wanted me to forgive her for some childish fight she'd had with Ona, she was crazy. If she felt bad about how she'd treated Ona, I wanted her to go on feeling bad. Ona had probably forgotten the whole episode, but it gave me a sweet sense of revenge to know Serena was suffering for some small cruelty she'd inflicted on my sister.

Then I just got tired of standing there: nothing makes you more tired than anger. I picked up my book bag and flung it over my shoulder. "Forget about it," I said. "Just leave us alone."

Everybody seemed to be watching me. I couldn't walk down Stockton Street without someone stopping me. Belle Char, who'd worked with Ona at Chinatown Bazaar, told me how she'd read about it in *The Chronicle.* Marc Chow, an old boyfriend I'd half forgotten about, said he couldn't believe it. "Ona always seemed . . . so cheerful." People called Salmon Alley; they dropped by the Baby Store. Some guy, I don't know who, called me at Mason's, but Mason hung up on him. Everybody knew they could find me at school, on yard duty. Tim Grange, a lecturer from City College, Emily Navarro, Lai-kay Lee, Chester Szeto, they all came to the school and talked to me through the chainlink fence; they all said they couldn't believe it. They all asked, Why?

How many dark mouths did I look into?

It was as though Ona was the one who made death real in their lives, and they all wanted to share their new knowledge with someone close to her. Talking to me gave them some kind of profound feeling they seemed to enjoy. But thank god I didn't have to listen to any more confessions. Everyone was sorry. They all wanted to know what they could do for me.

"Nothing," I said.

The oldtimers were easier to take. At least they brought gifts when they came by. Cousin and Croney Kam and Jimmy Lowe brought white gold in Ona's memory.

Croney remembered pushing Ona on the swings at Portsmouth Square. "How fast! How high, like flying." He rubbed his shoulder and moaned about how his arm used to hurt from pushing her. "Even I was afraid, watching her."

Jimmy taught her to play Twenty-one. "Smart kid, that Ona. Only one time I have to tell her. She remembered everything."

Cousin remembered that Leon used to take Ona to the chicken shop and that she loved to help pluck the birds. Chickens and ducks, pigeons and quails, sometimes a rare pheasant. "She had fast fingers," Croney said. "She had to stand on an overturned bucket to reach the high sinks, but she stood like that for hours, working on the bird till it was completely bald."

One day I took some lunch to Mah at the store. An ancient lady sat on a stool behind the counter. She leaned forward on her cane and called out, "Who's that?" I recognized her voice: a lilt, like singing. Then she called out my Chinese name and I remembered.

Ona called her Godmother, but I called her Auntie Wong. "Wong Moo, hello."

Out of respect for her age, I had to listen to her long lament for Ona. She brushed her palm across her eyes. She swayed on her cane. She told me she loved Ona more than her own blood grandchildren. She taught Ona how to eat rice, how to tie her shoes, how to sing songs. "I would have given her my own liver," she said.

She spoke our village dialect, and the sound of her voice made me want to cry. When she said "blood," I felt my blood. When she said "song," I heard singing. Her old voice—the long "aahhh" and sweet, soft "sshhh"— sounded elegiac. I could tell Wong Moo loved Ona.

So did Tommie Hom. I ran into him one lunch break when I went back to Salmon Alley to get the science papers I'd forgotten. When I turned the corner he was standing in front of his shop, smoking. I'd quit, but I couldn't resist one of Tommie's Kools. When he reached over to give me a light, I saw the age in his hands. The three of us were always wild about his gangster good looks. Ona especially loved the way he smoked. One summer, I remember, I wanted Mah to leave Leon and marry him.

Now, Tommie looked like an aging playboy.

He asked, "How's your Mah?"

"Not too good."

He looked down the alley toward our place.

I said, "But she opened the store."

"That's good."

When I inhaled on the harsh menthol cigarette, I felt my mean streak rise up. I said, "She blames herself, you know. Because of you."

He nodded slowly, giving his cigarette a practiced tap. "I know. I hear the ladies talk."

Tommie wasn't like Serena Choi; he would never ask my forgiveness. I said, "Leon blames you, too."

"I know," Tommie said. "He told me himself. In my own shop in front of all the ladies. Your father blames everybody. He has no shame."

"Stepfather."

Tommie shrugged. "He loves you like a father, that's all I know."

"He loved Ona."

With a flick of his finger, Tommie sent his cigarette flying toward Pacific Avenue. "We all loved her," he said. "Leon wasn't the only one."

THAT NIGHT was the first time since Ona jumped that I'd stayed away from Salmon Alley. But it didn't feel right. Something about the staying in the Mission felt like I was crashing out at somebody else's place.

I guess that's when I decided: Salmon Alley felt like the only safe place.

I packed my school materials and some clothes and drove everything over to Salmon Alley. It was the night of the New Year parade and the streets were crowded with tourists and vendors and kids selling firecrackers. As I carried my boxes up the stairs, I heard the slow, heavy beat of the drums. As I unpacked in my old room, the drums quickened like a pulse, and I remembered the times the three of us watched the dragon dancing down narrow Grant Avenue.

WONG MOO taught us an old village chant, a counting rhyme that matched ten living things to the first ten days of the New Year. When we were kids, we used this rhyme to count off each celebration day. Day one commemorated the chicken (it was Ona's year and she preferred calling it Phoenix), day two was for dogs, the third day for pigs, fourth for sheep, fifth for cows, and sixth for horses. Day seven was everybody's birthday; it was a feast day and we called it People Day. Day eight was for wheat and day nine was for soldiers. The tenth day was a day for thieves. Wong Moo told us, In this way all life was celebrated.

Now, I counted up to today. The Day of Thieves. Someone stole Ona. Ona hadn't wanted to go.

TEN

IN MY HEAD, the time around Ona's jump is a blur. Everything moved too fast or too slow. Time felt like a shove or a jerk.

The phone call. Going to the Vallejo Street police station. The way the Italian cop looked at me when he asked, Are you her sister? I felt sick, a fist in my stomach. My head pounded; everything felt raw. I had to see too much. I had too much to do. My hand shook when I signed where the policeman pointed. Pen. Paper. Press down.

Breathe, I kept telling myself, but I was afraid if I breathed I'd scream.

But moving through all this, simply and horribly, had its own comfort. I didn't have to think. I was carried by the momentum of events: walking into the Baby Store, Mah looking up calmly, the calm breaking to sobbing, her face hollow with shock, my arms around her narrow back, touching her head, stroking her hair.

Leon rushing up from the back of the store. Leon's questions, the same ones asked again and again, his asking and my answering like chanting.

This telling had a stillness, not time stopping, but time hurting.

MASON was there with me through all of it. The light felt heavy as slate when we got back to his place. I couldn't sleep. I kept asking why Ona chose the thirteenth floor. In our dialect, it was a good number. Thirteen sounds like "to live." Whenever I closed my eyes, I thought I heard Ona scream. In the back of my head, there was this low-pitched siren howling.

The whole next day felt unreal. All my senses were on full power. My sense of smell was especially acute. What I remember most of those first days was Leon's incense, the Lucky Fortune brand of sandalwood. Now the smell of it makes me feel faint.

Getting through the workday was the hardest. Lisa Chan, a fourth grader, reminded me of Ona. On yard duty, I watched her at Chinese jump rope, the slow way she raised her leg, tipped her head, slowly arched her back and pressed down for that last inch. It was Ona: her little leg and her supple back, and her arms swooping out, even how her tongue slipped out as she strained.

Everybody called. People Ona used to work with at Chinatown Bazaar, high school friends from Galileo. They wanted to talk. Nina suggested having people over to Salmon Alley on Sunday after the cremation, a service, something simple, a time for people to drop by. But Leon wanted a Chinese wake. Something fancy. He wanted to invite all his friends from the ships, shopowners, Mah's sewing-lady friends, his park-bench buddies. He talked about hiring an El Dorado, having Ona's poster-sized picture riding high above the cab for everyone to see. He wanted to take Ona for her last walk. He wanted to hire a professional wailer. He wanted to fill all of Chinatown with his grief.

Nina rolled her eyes and said she didn't want any of that hocus-pocus, which sent Leon onto a rant about Confucian rites. When he warned about ancestral retribution and Nina muttered, "What ancestor?" Leon was so pissed off he blamed everything on Mah and said, "Just like you, no manners, bad home education." Mah called Leon a do-nothing bum. He called her a bad mother, the world's worst wife. I tried to stay out of it, but when Nina shouted at them to shut up, I yelled at Nina to show more respect.

If Mason hadn't been there, if he hadn't stood up and said, "Okay, enough," who knows, we'd probably slugged it out.

Mason said, "Okay, this is what we're gonna do. We're gonna split up the jobs."

I remember the quiet then: I remember scowling into my lap. I heard Nina mutter, Oh brother.

Mason asked her to pick up the ashes.

Nina said nothing.

I looked up at her but couldn't see her face; she had her head bowed and her hair fell forward, hiding her expression.

She nodded.

I heard Mah's tentative voice asking Leon what he was going to wear. She was worried that Leon might wear his gangster suit.

Leon walked out.

ALTHOUGH Miss Lagomarsino told me to take whatever time I needed, I couldn't afford it; we had parent-teacher conferences.

By Thursday, I was beat. Since Nina was home, I was staying in the Mission. Mason said he'd arranged to meet Leon at Portsmouth Square at four. They were going to go shopping for something to wear. I said I'd try to track Leon down after school let out, to remind him.

Mason stopped me midsentence, "Lei, leave him alone, okay?"

I was shocked at the way he said my name, low-toned and worried.

"What do you mean?" I asked. "I want to make sure he remembers."

I heard myself sounding like Nina, defensive.

"He'll remember." Mason shook his head in that way that meant everything, but I knew just by the way he was standing that he wasn't going to talk about it.

I stood there for a while longer, trying to think of something to say. But nothing came out. I knew he was upset about my coming and going. Maybe it was even as simple as his being mad that I was going to stay on Salmon Alley that night.

I tried to think of something to say besides "Sorry." Mason *hates* it; he says I use that word too much.

He said, "Take the Fiat, I gotta work on your car."

"What's wrong?"

"The clutch is going."

I picked up my stuff, wanting to ask if he was mad at me. "You gonna call me?"

"Later."

Mason told me to leave Leon alone, not to go looking for him. But I couldn't help it. I was all nerves, and I felt like if I didn't personally touch everything it would fall apart.

After school, I went looking for him at the Universal, and found him sitting at the counter reading the paper. I slipped in next to him, said Hi. He just nodded.

"You're meeting Mason at four, right?"

He nodded again.

"You're coming to the service, aren't you?"

He gave me a look and then went back to his paper.

I sat there for a while. Even though I didn't get much of an answer out of Leon, just seeing him made me feel better. If he didn't show, it wasn't my fault.

I headed back toward my car, but Chinatown felt claustrophobic, so I drove down to the Wharf; but that reminded me of all the times we came down here to say goodbye to Leon. I wanted to be near water so I headed toward the Marina. When I saw the kites in the air and the sailboats in the distance and the gray mound that was Alcatraz, I felt better. Then the big Safeway came into view and I remembered all the stuff I had to pick up for the service, and I pulled into the lot. Coke and 7-Up and juice and coffee and paper stuff, the plates and cups and spoons. I threw house-cleaning things into the cart, too. I put the bags into the trunk and then walked next door to Discount Liquors for some empty boxes. The Fiat was stuffed.

When I pulled up to Salmon Alley, I felt armed. I felt like I was going to accomplish something. I wanted to clear out Ona's clothes, get her things packed and boxed and put away down in the basement. I guess I was nervous about being left alone with the job. I wanted Nina to help me, and I wanted to do it before the service.

I didn't want to throw anything of Ona's away; I wasn't ready to go through it. Even looking at Ona's handwriting upset me. I didn't want to find anything that might tell me why she jumped.

Nina's clothes were all over the bedroom, which made me nervous; I didn't want to get any of Ona's things mixed up with Nina's. I started with Ona's dresser, pulling the drawers all the way out and dumping everything into the liquor boxes. Then I went to the closet and grabbed wide armfuls of dresses and jackets and lifted them off the rod. I stuffed them, hangers and all, into black plastic garbage sacks.

Nina came in as I emptied out the closet. She seemed mad, and I was just about to say, Don't worry, I'm not touching your stuff, when she said, "Mah! She drives me nuts. I'm glad I'm leaving. I wish I were going tonight, I swear!"

"She can't be any worse than Leon," I said.

"At least he doesn't whine. He doesn't do a boo-hoo-hoo number. You should've seen her. I dropped by the Baby Store with the ashes and Mah acted like she didn't want them in the store. There were all these sewing ladies, you know, Luday, Soon-ping, Gordon's Mom, and even Miss Tsai—guess what! she got fat! They were all giving Mah a sympathy visit, and when Mah saw the urn, she freaked and grabbed it from me and slipped it under the register like she was hiding it. She's so weird! The ladies saw. I mean, it wasn't like she was slick or anything. They saw. And they knew. By now, probably everybody in Chinatown knows."

"Why'd she hide it?" I asked.

"Tommie Hom! For Mah, everything goes back to that. Mah thinks she's paying for Tommie Hom. That's why she's being so weird to Leon."

"That's ridiculous! She can't be holding on to that."

"You weren't there. You should've seen her. She was scared of those ladies."

"Nina, you are so weird."

"Don't believe me, then. She thinks everything has to do with Tommie Hom. You living with Mason. Me in New York. Leon at the San Fran. Ona jumping is only the worst thing. Everything's connected to Tommie, connected by those gossipmongers."

I shook my head and started lugging Ona's things into the hall. Nina followed me.

"Ask her. Go ahead, get screamed at like me."

"Tommie was over ten years ago."

"Tell Mah," Nina said.

"And anyway. It doesn't have anything to do with Ona. Why she jumped."

"Don't tell me. Tell Mah." Nina didn't want to talk anymore about Ona.

MASON called late, after midnight. He said he'd had a crazy time tracking Leon down. Leon didn't show at the Square, and Mason had to run around asking about him. Finally, he got Cousin to talk by buying him a couple of beers at Red's Place. Turns out Leon booked himself on a three-day gamblers' special to Reno and he was scheduled to leave at midnight. Cousin said he was hanging around with Jimmy at the Lowe family association, practicing blackjack. Mason waited at the bus stop until Leon showed up.

"It wasn't easy, but I talked him out of it. He's here now; we're drinking scotch. Watching boxing."

"Let me talk to him," I said.

"No," Mason said. "He's all right. Zeke says his dad and Leon are about the same size. He'll bring a suit over in the morning. Don't worry."

But I worried and I had a hard time falling asleep. Ona was gone. Nina was going away. Already I felt lonely. Leon and Mason were clear across town, and all evening Mah kept to herself, staying at the other end of the apartment, watching me and Nina go up and down the back stairs with Ona's boxes. I didn't talk to her, so I don't know what was going on in her head. All I knew was that she wasn't looking forward to the service; none of us were.

None of us even wanted to think about Ona's being dead. Mah worried about her affair with Tommie Hom, but it was Ona. Nina couldn't wait to get away from us, from Chinatown, but it was Ona. I thought all I wanted was to get out of Salmon Alley, to live in the Mission with Mason, but it was Ona. Who knows what went through Leon's head? Easy money. Easy win. An easy way to win Ona back.

I heard all the old alley sounds—Old Mr. Lim's cough coming through the wall, Mrs. Lim going for his medicine, and outside, the long foghorn, the rumble of Ernie Chang's Camaro—it must have been way after two. Hearing those old sounds soothed me. They made Salmon Alley comfortable again. I felt cocoon-safe in the old sounds, in the homey feeling of time standing still. I remembered the three of us in this room together, giggling and crying and fighting and making up. Four thin walls and a world of feeling.

I wasn't ready to say goodbye to Ona.

None of us were ready. Ona was dead before we had a chance to save her. We hadn't had time to catch up. To let go, I know we had to let our memories out.

I remember Ona with my back. The summer before culottes became popular, Ona and I were a tight team, helping Mah sew dozens of the hot-pink and neon-green skirts at home. Ona stood behind my chair waiting for the pockets, which she turned, and for the interfacing, which she ironed.

Ona liked to play a risky game. She waited till I was sewing fast, gunning the motor; and then her hand would come flying over my shoulder and slap at the whirling belt. It drove me crazy. I reminded her about how Repairman Loy's arm got dragged into the churning motors by his loose sleeve. Your fingers are like sleeves, I warned. Ona only laughed. She wasn't scared. Ona did it for fun. She loved the fun of getting close to the danger and the thrill of getting away.

Other memories broke through, making it hard to fall asleep. I knew Nina still felt guilty about the time she got Ona in trouble. Ona was twelve, so Nina must have been ten. They weren't allowed to leave Chinatown without permission, but Ona often went downtown with her friends anyway. Once Mah came home early from work and Ona wasn't home yet. Nina tattled; Mah locked Ona out. That evening, Nina sat in her room listening to Ona screaming.

Mason saved Ona from making a fool of herself once. It was after Byron Tang dumped her and she was at a party, getting wasted on Q's and Tom Collinses. Mason was there, too, and he kept an eye on her. When he saw that she was going to get sick soon, he went over and offered to take her home. He put her in his borrowed BMW and shut the door. By the time he got around to his side, she'd puked. He never did get her puke smell out of that car.

Poor Leon lost Ona once, way back when she was still wearing bells on her shoes. He said that she kept pulling away, wanting to walk alone. So he let her go on her own.

When he didn't hear the bells and couldn't remember when last he had, he retraced his steps, checking every Chinatown shop he'd stopped in. But no Ona.

Ona was in Hop Sing's, having a fun tour of the big refrigerators, where she touched a floppy pig ear and saw pig snouts and cow tongues. A butcher showed her how he twisted the square of pink paper into a smooth cone container. He carried her into a room with whistling blades and showed her an oxtail cut into chunks. She liked his pink apron, his banana-fat fingers and his big hands. So big, she told us, that sitting in them felt like sitting in a swing. The butcher recognized Ona as the pretty seamstress's little girl and called Tommie Hom's factory. Mah was working to make a deadline, so it was Tommie who came for Ona.

Leon was out at sea when Ona was born, so Mah named her herself. But Mah was thinking of Leon when she picked the name Ona. Leon/Ona. *On* was part of Leon's Chinese name, too. It means "peace" in our dialect. Mah said it seemed respectful as well as hopeful. Leon was her new man and Ona was their new baby.

Ona. I lay in bed saying the name to myself. Ona. Trying to get the sound right. Ona. Trying to remember how Mah said it, the long *o* sound, the soft *ahhhh* sounding like a surprise.

In the morning, Mah went off early to have her hair done at Duckie's Mom's. I walked down to Great Eastern for our order of dim sum. When I got back, Nina'd set up the long table for the food and arranged the mantle with pictures and fresh flowers. I made the tea and coffee and filled the thermoses.

Cousin was the first one to arrive, looking a little sheepish for ruining Leon's Reno trip. Croney Kam came with

Jimmy Lowe, who acted like he'd rather be playing the slot machines. Meilian Jue and her husband, Dennis, came with their two-year-old. Priscilla Toy, Dorothy Chew, Emilia Valdez, and Keiko Muramoto came in a group and left together after about fifteen minutes. Kevin Lum looked the same with his long hair and wispy mustache. He told me that Leland Huie was in jail.

Even Tommie Hom showed up. Nina said it looked like he'd ratted his hair; she thought he looked like a Chinese Elvis. He must have smoked a dozen cigarettes leaning against the mantle. Every time I offered him food, he just shook his head and lit up another smoke.

The circle was complete—except for Osvaldo. I knew he wouldn't come, but still I half hoped he would. I appreciated his way of thinking; he knew his being there would make it harder on everyone.

The mood was odd. People came up to me, scared to be happy and scared to be sad. Simple smiles. A couple of times, I heard Zeke laughing. I even thought I heard someone say, "Happy New Year."

Mah had cried so much the last few days the salt traced lines down her cheek. She was still crying, but the sewing ladies kept coaching her: "Talk. Talk good things and urge the sadness away." So I was glad to see Mimi Fong, Ona's best friend from grade school, talking to Mah. I heard Mimi say in English, "You had a nice daughter."

I looked up and saw Mah blink. She answered back in English. "Three nice daughters."

PEOPLE everywhere. Nina and I passed each other with trays of food and gave each other I-can't-believe-we're-doing-this looks. I went looking for Zeke, to thank him for loaning Leon the suit. He was in the kitchen, giving Meilian advice on how to buy a used car. Diana asked me about my job, and I was telling her about my new position when the sewing ladies came breezing toward me, a blow of perfume, puffs of bouffant hair, dumpling faces, eyebrows arched in brown pencil. Their soft necks bent as they paid condolences. I thanked them for coming, took their outstretched hands. I kissed their powdery cheeks. They chirped village ditties at me. I nodded, letting the rhymes work their comforting charms. I patted their hands, complimented their sincerity, their good, big hearts, even their big hair. I watched Miss Tsai go down the rickety steps in her high heels. When she turned back to wave, I couldn't resist and singsonged after her, "Walk carefully!"

Finally it was over. Leon left with Cousin and Jimmy Lowe and I didn't even ask where they were going. I'd noticed Nina flirting with Kevin and half thought she'd go out for drinks with him, but her mind was already in New York, I guess. She stayed and helped me clean up and then went to the bedroom to pack. Mason stretched out on the couch and crashed out, waiting to drive Nina to the airport at midnight. Mah said she was too tired to go and went to bed.

I finished up in the kitchen and then went into the living room and plopped into Leon's fat-man chair. I just sat there, watching Mason sleep. It looked so good, so easy. I was so tired, I couldn't even think. But one word kept coming back into my head.

Why. Why. Why. Why. Why?

ELEVEN

I WAS at the back of the room getting everything set up for the afternoon art class: scissors, glue and glitter, the construction paper. The kids were at their desks doing their math assignments, but they kept glancing back at the skeleton of the red-and-gold dragon I'd tacked up on the bulletin board. I could hear paper rustling and Lisa Chan whispering and chairs scraping on the floor—work sounds.

But then I heard something like a sigh, like sound falling away, and it got quiet. The class became strangely still. I turned and saw the kids staring at the door.

At Miss Lagomarsino. I recognized the look on her face. It was the same look she had when she came to tell me that Alvin Joe's father had cut his thumb off at the Hop Sing butcher shop. Miss Lagomarsino had her emergency face on, but I could tell it wasn't an earthquake or fire drill she wanted to talk about.

"Miss Fu," she said. She backed away from the door and disappeared.

The next thing I knew, I was in the hall. It was cool and quiet out there. Miss Lagomarsino was talking to me, but I can't remember anything she actually said, only that she wouldn't stop talking. Her words kept piling up, another and another, each one a heavy stone. Even her presence, the physical mass of her, was a pressure. It felt like she was too tall, too wide, and just too big, that she was standing too close to me; all I could think about was taking a step back, but I was afraid of being rude. She towered over me and then she seemed to loom closer. I saw the powdered pores around her nostrils, the quiver of her lip when she finally stopped talking. I saw the pale center of her eyes cloud. It felt like I was sitting in the front row at a movie; I could see everything, but I was too close to see the whole picture. I saw flashes, edges. Things blurred. My eyes were skimming the surface. I couldn't take it all in, the total picture that my sister was dead.

The police, Miss Lagomarsino said. The Vallejo Street station. The words came out of a white gate of teeth. For the first time, I realized that her teeth were false.

She led me to her office. Someone gave me a chair. Someone said, Drink. I held the cup. I could feel the coolness of the water through the paper. I drank. The cold news was inside me now.

I saw Ona falling and falling. She wouldn't stop: it was like movement and no movement. I sipped. The water brought my breath back. I was suspended between air and water, breathing and crying. I took a deep breath. Breathing in, I felt hollow. I heard metal taps on the marble floors, a peculiar rhythm, a drag and then a click. It was Miss O'Shea's polio gait.

MISS LAGOMARSINO said I could take whatever time I needed. I remember that the word "thanks" was in my head. I might have nodded.

Time rushed ahead, swelling, and then snapped still, stopping. It reminded me of the time Mason and I had snorted heroin. We were cruising and when we came to a stop, probably only for a minute at the most, that minute felt like forever. It felt like I'd drifted to the slow edge of the world, where time froze, then became liquid and then vapor. I felt the car's slow vibration. I watched the red light drop two spots and turn green.

The recess bell rang, a high, insistent, stabbing sound. I heard the heavy doors open, a wave of voices. Sneakers squeaking. A ball bounced. Laughter. A warning shh! Then I heard the doors slam, one by one, down the hallway.

I walked out of the office, down the stairs, and into the girl's bathroom. Inside, I felt refrigerator-safe. I wanted to sink into the coolness, to freeze time. I locked myself in a stall, sat down on the edge of the toilet and put my head on my lap. Oh god. My whisper filled the tight space, beating the god word back at me. God. God. God. I slapped the roll of toilet paper and watched the sheets billow out and gather in white waves at my feet.

I remembered the time I went in there and found Ona crying. For two years we were at Edith Eaton together. One afternoon I found her hiding in a stall, crying, her socks around her ankles, her dress a mess. I didn't ask why she was crying; I only scolded her for ruining the dress Mah had stayed up all night to finish.

Why didn't I ask? Why was I more concerned with Mah than with Ona?

Mah always made Ona and Nina dresses from the same pattern. She liked to dress Ona in white and Nina in red.

Now, I saw Ona's white dress, its scalloped neckline, the puffy sleeves, the long sash bow in the back. I knew every part of that dress. I remembered the bolt of fabric on the table at National Dollar Store and how the lady cut the yardage with one long pass of the scissors she wore like a necklace, and the fabric soaking in the bathtub at home and drying on our roof, the bright smell of wind on it as I took it down and folded it into squares. Mah laid the fabric on the kitchen table. The pattern was a scaled-down version of the dress they were sewing at Tommie's. Mah used pig-pink butcher paper from Hop Sing's. I sat at my dinner place and watched her cut out the dress. She let me sew the long sash on the Singer, and while I turned and pressed it, she sewed the dress front to the dress back and worked on the neckline and the sleeves. I kept her company till way past midnight while she hemmed the new white dress. Mah hung the perfect and pressed white dress right above Ona's bed so that it would be the first thing she saw.

I should have asked Ona, Why are you crying? What are you sad about? I wish I'd hugged her, kissed her cheeks. But I hadn't, and now I can hear Mah asking, Where did you learn such meanness?

I looked up through the tunnel of the stall at the ceiling light, thinking, I have to tell Mah and Leon. A shot of fear and then another shot of recognition ran through me. There I was, hiding in the restroom, just like Ona.

I left the lavatory and climbed the stairs and slipped out the side doors. Outside, the light was aggressive. Every shining surface caught the sun: the chainlink fence, car mirrors, windows, street signs, a man's watch, parking meters, water running in the gutter, the flash of a woman's glasses. I felt chased by it; the light hurt my eyes and I kept blinking.

On Stockton Street, everything seemed speeded up. An Impala ran a red light. The bus lurched to a stop. People moved with the jerky motion of puppets. I walked against the rush, feeling casual—no groceries, no purse, no books, not even a sweater—almost as if my being outside were an accident. I wasn't in a rush. I wanted to believe I had all the time in the world. I never wanted to get to the police station.

And then I was there. On Vallejo Street.

A row of cars were lined up for the garage. Next door, powder-blue cop cars were pulled up onto the sidewalk in front of the station. As I walked in, I hoped crazily to see a line in there, too, but of course there wasn't one.

The first cop I talked to wouldn't tell me anything. He said, "Wait," and got up from his desk and went into another room. I watched him go. Should I stand or sit? I looked behind me and saw a row of black plastic chairs along the wall. A telephone booth. Did I have enough time to call Mason? Did I have a quarter? I patted my skirt pocket, then reached in and felt my coin purse. But I thought, No. Talking to Mason would open up too much. There wasn't enough time. I felt awkward about standing around but I couldn't get myself to move toward the black chairs on the far side of the room, so I leaned against the counter until the rookie cop came back out and motioned for me.

I followed the stencil-blue back of his shirt into a sun-bright office. Through the window, I saw children's clothes hanging on the fire escape across the alley, and I thought of Mah at the Baby Store. A bald cop sat behind a desk. The flag in the corner made me feel like I was in Miss Lagomarsino's office again.

Nothing the cop asked or said about Ona bothered me; I had ready answers for everything. No, there were no previous attempts. No, I had no clues about this coming on. Yes, I knew about the drugs. There was a boyfriend, Osvaldo Ong, but they broke up. A while back. No, he wasn't involved in a gang. She was taking some classes at City College. She worked nights at The Traders. Yes, the same one that had been in Oakland. She lived on Salmon Alley. No fights. No problems out of the ordinary. No hints. Nothing.

He didn't get it. He was looking at the typical stuff. He was looking at now. Maybe I could have said something about how Ona felt stuck. In the family, in Chinatown. Ona was the middle girl and she felt stuck in the middle of all the trouble.

I could have given him Leon's explanation that it was because Grandpa Leong's bones weren't at rest. Or Mah's, that it was as simple as Ona feeling betrayed no one came to her rescue about Osvaldo, that she had to suffer the blame for Ong & Leong's failure.

But I didn't say any of this; it wasn't anything he could use for his report. Besides, it started to get on my nerves that he called me Miss; that he couldn't understand why Ona and I had different last names. Bringing Mah and Leon into it wouldn't explain anything; talking about them always confused things; I didn't have any ready answers about them. I mumbled that it was a long story. "We're sisters," I said.

The cop's questions reminded me of the time Ona got caught shoplifting at Woolworth's. I went with Leon to pick her up. Leon understood enough English, but he had me translate all the manager's questions for him anyway. Leon's tone didn't need translation. He jutted his chin at the man, practically shouting, "What's the big deal? It's only lipstick. No big deal." He kept calling the manager names: White Devil, Crooked-Nose, Liar. I had to cover for Leon and get him out of there as quickly as possible.

Ona was locked in the manager's closet-sized office. I was surprised when he opened the door. Ona looked as calm and rested as if she were lifting her head from a nap. I'd expected to see a face full of fear or relief, but Ona looked like Little Miss No-Big-Deal. She was nine, maybe ten. The man let her go with a warning, "Don't let me catch you again."

Afterward, Leon took us for ice-cream sundaes at Fong Fong Brothers. We sat in a lipstick-red booth, scooping half-melted ice cream into our mouths, like cool soup. Leon had a banana split. He told us, "Don't tell Mah. Our secret. It was only a little thing. Only lipstick."

The cop wrote out an address for me, but he seemed to hold the slip back a moment, saying something about more forms and verification, identification.

"I'm sorry," he said.

I said yes, and pushed out of my chair.

I found the phone booth in the hall. When I folded the door closed, time slowed again. I sat. I found my coin purse and opened it. It bloomed open. The dull coins fascinated me. They felt cool as wet stones as I counted them. All I needed was a quarter to call Mason, but the crumpled bills and the flat circles—quarters, nickels, the five shiny dimes—added up to something. It was simple. For that moment, they were all I had in the world and they were all I needed. I could call Mason and buy a cup of cappuccino.

Jorge answered and yelled for Mason. While I waited I could hear the hollow gonglike sounds of the shop, the rock and roll in the background.

"Yeah? Lei?" Something about hearing his voice made me lose it; I started crying and it got worse and worse. It

got so bad I had to put the phone down and dry my face
with my sleeve.

"What happened? Lei?"

"Ona," I said.

"What?"

"She jumped."

"She what?"

"Off the Nam."

"God."

"I can't believe it."

"Lei."

"It's awful."

"Is she . . . I mean, where is she?"

"She's dead."

"Lei."

"I know."

"Where are you?"

"Vallejo."

"Wait for me."

"Not here. I don't want to stay here."

I WALKED down the block, to wait at Caffe Venezia,
but it was closed. I looked at my watch and saw that it was
only a little past ten. I cupped my hands to the window and
peered in, looking for Ivo or Antonella. Nothing moved in
the shadows. All I could see was the bright traffic flashing
by in the mirror behind the bar.

I sat down on the stoop to wait. Mah would say I
looked like a beggar girl, but I didn't care. It felt good to
sit in the sun for a while, and I knew I wouldn't have to
wait long. The Mission's not that far, twenty minutes,

maybe half an hour with midmorning traffic, but the way Mason drives, I expected to see him turn up Stockton in his Camaro any minute.

A man was selling doghouse-size blocks of toilet tissue off the back of his flatbed truck. His sign said THIRTEEN DOLLARS. Baby carriages rolled by, their handles bright with orange and yellow plastic grocery bags.

Then, coming up the street, a cluster of old guys. I could tell from their pace they were the dangerous type: talkers, wanderers, time wasters. I looked for Leon in their group. He wasn't with them this time and I was relieved; it would've been awful for him to find me, sitting on some stoop, looking like a beggar. Besides, I wasn't ready to tell yet.

But when Mason's Camaro pulled up, I slipped in and, without even thinking about it, said, "The Baby Store." Mason kept the car moving through the traffic. He didn't say anything. He looked like he'd just crawled out from under a car. He had a wrench in his pocket and his hair was still tied back with a rubber band and his hands were greasy. A gray streak ran from his earlobe almost to the corner of his mouth.

I was never so glad to see him.

Mason pulled all four wheels onto the sidewalk and cut the engine. He looked at me close for the first time and I leaned over and pressed my forehead against his neck. I smelled his faint metal scent.

"Want me to come in?"

I shook my head. "I'm okay."

Grant Avenue glittered like a Hollywood movie set. As I passed Mah's carousel pony, I touched its old worn head—my superstitious habit—and pushed through the double glass doors. I was inside. The string of bells jingled, then everything was still. No opera, no coffee aroma, not a single customer. Mah was in the front by the register, Leon in the back holding an armful of dresses. I glimpsed their surprised expressions at seeing me. Time stood dead-still.

I just said it. "Ona. Ona's dead. *Mo* Ona, no more Ona. She jumped off the Nam Ping Yuen. Ona *tui-low.* The police told me."

I felt the shock fresh, hearing the news out of my own mouth, all mixed up in English, Chinese.

"What?"

"What?"

They both stared at me the same way.

My throat burned from telling. I didn't want to say it again.

And then Mah just crumpled to the floor.

"MahMahMah!" I dropped down and gathered her in my arms. Our cheeks touched.

"My daughter, my daughter," she wailed.

I knelt there and rocked her until she was quiet. Leon helped me pull her to her feet. Mah hid her face against my shoulder as I walked her outside. Mason was by the car, but when he saw us, he stepped forward and Mah surprised me by reaching for him. Leon was right behind me and I told him to go on with Mah, that I'd lock up.

"You got the keys?" I held my hand out for them.

He fished in his pockets and dropped the heavy ring into my hand and then climbed into the car.

I just stared at the metal clump in my hand. I couldn't believe all the keys sticking out in all directions. I felt the grime and grease and metal and then just the plain confusion. I got more and more upset. There must have been twenty, twenty-five keys on that ring. What the hell were they all for? I picked through the bunch but none of them were labeled. It was crazy: what did he do? Save every key to every lock in his life? I closed my hand over the jagged clump and went right up to the car and rapped on the window. Leon looked up out of the dark backseat. I made a churning motion with my fist that meant, Roll the window down. I shouted out, "Which one?"

He looked at me with a blank expression, as if he didn't hear me.

I said again, "Which key?!" I shoved the key ring into the car; I didn't realize my force, but I dropped it. The whole metal clump landed in his lap.

I heard Leon mumbling.

And then Mah's voice, "This. And this one."

"All right," I said, and went back to the store.

I checked the back door: locked. The coffee machine and rice cooker were unplugged. No money in the register, so I left the drawer wide open. I hit the lights, flipped the sign to CLOSED and locked up.

When I got into the car, I glanced back at Mah and Leon and was shocked at how scared they looked, pressed deep into the dark seats like they were trying to hide. I was glad to feel the car's vibration, to hear the soothing hum.

Mason eased the car back onto the road and we were off. We slid along Grant Avenue, gliding.

From the low seats of the Camaro, I looked out at the streets and saw the spidery writing on the store signs, the dressed-up street lamps with their pagoda tops, the oddly matched colors: red with green, green with aqua blue, yellow with pink.

Looking out, I thought, So this is what Chinatown looks like from inside those dark Greyhound buses; this slow view, these strange color combinations, these narrow streets, this is what tourists come to see. I felt a small lightening up inside, because I knew, no matter what people saw, no matter how close they looked, our inside story is something entirely different. I knew the dangers of closing up, but I didn't care. Right then, I didn't want people looking in at us. I wanted to slide down deeper into myself; I wanted to hide from everything. I'd dreaded telling Mah and Leon, and now it was done. I dreaded telling Nina, but that too would soon be over with, and then what? What would we do after the telling? We'd bury Ona; we'd mourn Ona. And then what?

After Grandpa Leong died, Leon told us that sorrow moves through the heart the way a ship moves through the ocean. Ships are massive, but the ocean has simple superiority. Leon described the power: One mile forward and eight miles back.

Forward and forward and then back, back.

Inside all of us, Ona's heart still moves forward. Ona's heart is still counting, true and truer to every tomorrow.

MASON pulled into Salmon Alley and stopped right in front of our apartment. As I walked in, the first thing I saw was Ona's unmade bed, the covers thrown back, the slippers crisscrossed on the floor, and I felt my back tense up. I rushed past.

I heard Leon behind me, mumbling something Chinese. Leon had held Mah's hand in the car, he had supported her coming up the stairs, and now he was leading her down the hallway to the living room. Mah crumpled onto the couch and started sobbing.

Their reactions were the complete opposite of what I'd expected. Already mourning, Mah seemed to begin to accept it. Leon would not. His questions started as soon as Mason closed the door on Salmon Alley. I walked into the kitchen to get Mah a glass of water. I turned the water on full and let it run. But I could still hear him.

What happened? What time? Why would she jump? Are you sure somebody didn't push her? Did somebody give her drugs?

I said nothing. Silence was safer. I rinsed off a glass and filled it. I took the water to Mah, but she just shook her head.

"Tea, then?"

Mah shook her head.

"Just boiled water?" suggested Mason.

Mah nodded.

"I'll take care of it," Mason said.

Leon kept on: "But I just talked to her last night. Last night, I tell you. We even laughed. I told a joke and she laughed. She said we were going to go shopping this weekend. Go to Alameda Fleamarket. She said so. Last night. I tell you. She was okay. She didn't tell me anything was wrong."

I purposely did not look at Leon. I knew he was sitting by Mah, on the arm of the fat-man chair. I imagined that he might have been hitting his chest to make a point, but I didn't look because I was afraid to see his face.

He went on, "She would have told me, I'm her father."

All I remember is feeling sorry for him right then. I wanted to tell him to stop it, but I couldn't say it. I tried to tune him out.

But Leon kept insisting, "She's my daughter, I'm her father. Why wouldn't she tell her father if something was wrong? She was okay. I would know these things. Besides she was only twenty, a girl. Where would a girl like her get an idea like that? Jumping off a building, I just cannot believe it. That no-good Ong boy must have something to do with it."

Leon's saying Osvaldo's name reminded me of the emergency siren sounding off at school. We'd trained the children to react immediately when they heard the siren: Dive under the table, hold your head down. The sound of Osvaldo's name had the same effect. Mah's head jerked up. Mason stepped out of the kitchen. Everything went completely still. But none of us knew how to protect ourselves.

Leon repeated the name again for effect. "Osvaldo!" He picked up on our anxiety, and walked across the room to the telephone. He demanded, "What's his number?"

I tried to hold my temper.

"I call him," Leon said, and it seemed more meditative, as if he were trying to call up the courage in himself. "I call him. I ask him."

I said, "Leave him out of it."

Leon had already picked up the phone. When he looked at me, it was all challenge. "What's his number? Give me his number."

"Leave him out of it," I said. "He had nothing to do with it. They broke up!" I knew I should stop there, but I couldn't. "Remember? You don't remember? You guys made her."

Leon put the phone down and walked right over to me. At first I was afraid he was going to hit me. Mason must have sensed something because I saw him coming into the living room, his wet hands, one cupped inside the palm of the other, looking like resting fists. But when Leon got closer, I saw that his face was full of shock and hurt and anger, all the stuff I felt but was trying to hold back.

He wagged his finger at me. His mouth was moving, but the only thing that came out was "You, you, you . . . you . . . you!"

Mah reacted by wailing louder and then running out of the room. Leon followed her after casting a scowl at me.

The kettle whistled but I didn't move. I heard cabinet doors open and shut.

Leon came back into the living room. He didn't face me; he didn't even say my name. He roared at the room, at the four walls. He went into his variation on three or four themes: Going back to China, only a bowl of bitterness to show for his life as a coolie. No one grateful. No one compassionate. I worried that he might start in on Mah and Tommie, but he didn't. He damned the day Luciano Ong came to Chinatown.

Leon's ranting. Leon's noise. Leon's nonsense. I tried not to take anything he said to heart. What Leon was really saying was that everything and everyone had disappointed him. My way of dealing with him when he was like that was just to ignore him. But it was hard to ignore his thumping back and forth in his heavy lead-toed army boots, his warpath from the kitchen to the living room, down the hallway to the bedroom and back again. There was something about how Leon was using English that was making me nervous.

Finally, he marched into the kitchen where Mason was and started in on him.

"What do you think happened? You think that Ong boy, that half-Spaniard, had anything to do with it? That Osvaldo, he a fool-around, yeah?"

"Osvaldo was okay," Mason said.

It was quiet. Leon seemed to be thinking about what Mason said. I was thinking about how strange it was that Leon was using English.

In English Leon started again: "I mean, Ona not that kind of girl. She talk to me first. I'm her father. She tell her father first, if something was wrong. Somebody put idea in her head. She talk to you, eh? Say something maybe?"

Mason didn't say anything, he just let Leon talk, run off with his questions.

Leon pressed him. "Police tell you something? Who found her?"

I couldn't take it and got up and went into Mah's room. She was lying on top of the covers, staring up at the ceiling.

I stepped up to her and whispered, "Mah?"

She didn't answer, didn't even look over at me.

Close up, I saw her tears. I heard her weeping.

"Mah?" I said again.

She rolled away from me and faced the wall. I sat down at the foot of the bed to wait. I heard Mason's voice, muted, patient: The police don't know. Then I heard Leon's voice, but I couldn't make out what he was saying in his half-English, half-Chinese speech.

The heavy footsteps came down the hall, stopping in front of the bedroom. He pushed the door open a crack. He called her by her name but Mah didn't even blink.

He said, "I'm going to the police station, I'm going to find out."

I got up and rushed after him, catching up to him on the stairs.

"Leon!" I called out. "Leon, wait!"

He didn't answer, didn't even turn around, though I called and called his name. So I made a grab for his elbow.

I got a snatch of his shirt sleeve but he jerked his elbow and flung my hand off. Then he charged down the rest of the stairs into the alley.

Mason was at the door. "Let him go."

I watched Leon stamping down the alley.

I felt more and more nervous. I just knew Leon was going to make a mess, stir up some trouble outside.

"He'll be okay," Mason said. "He'll come back by himself."

"What? Like a dog?" I slammed the door behind me and stood there remembering the many other times I came home to find Leon gone, signed onto some voyage without telling us.

Mah once explained that it was the movement of the ocean that drew him out, made him restless on land. Staying on land too long made Leon feel like he was turning to stone. The ocean was his whole world: complete. A rush of wind and water. The salt taste like endless crying. What opens for him in the hollow and still center of the ocean?

I remembered the word: Completion.

I saw Ona flying. Somewhere, I was circling after her, but I couldn't follow. I heard her catching laugh and then the struggling sounds of her sobbing, and suddenly, the news about Ona dying came rushing back at me.

Another word came: Escape.

What Leon searched for, what Ona needed.

Then I saw Mason motioning to me from outside Mah's room. He handed me the mug of hot water. I went in and offered it to Mah, but she didn't answer, so I put it on her dresser and then sat down at the foot of her bed, waiting. Mason came in and sat with me.

Mah said she felt nervous. It was like she chose a foreign word to express a foreign feeling in the hopes of keeping it far from her. Noi-vay-see. Mah said the word in three syllables, stretching out the anger, the despair, and the sadness that were welling up inside her.

Mason thought it sounded like Courvoisier and said it might be good to give her some.

I said I needed it more.

Then Mah asked for Nina. She said, "I want all my daughters home."

TELLING Nina over long distance was harder than I expected. Nina was living in New York with this new guy, but she hadn't told Mah and Leon the whole story yet. She hadn't even told me the whole story. I didn't know his name, so when he answered the phone, I just asked for Nina.

"Nina just stepped out," he said.

I told him it was an emergency. "Tell her to call her sister," I said. "I'm in Chinatown."

Ten, fifteen minutes, Nina called right back. Everything Nina said—or didn't say—bothered me. I interpreted her quiet as not wanting to come. I'd been worried about Mah and Leon and I hadn't given myself the time to feel. But telling Nina and hearing her response slowed everything down and I felt my loss for the first time. I'd lost my sister.

"When you coming back?"

The line was quiet.

Then Nina's voice. Faint. "I don't know."

I didn't say anything. To me it was as if she'd said, Do I have to? I knew it wasn't that Nina didn't want to, it had something to do with our way of talking. That I assumed she'd come, expected it. She didn't like my questions and I hated her stubborn, shut-off silence.

The phone rang again right after I hung up. It was Sergeant Kilpatrick from the Vallejo precinct saying that Leon was there, very upset, could somebody come for him? I was glad Mason offered to go.

NINA'S flight was due in at eight-thirty. I didn't want to drive by and pick her up at the curbside; it seemed too casual. I wanted to get there early. I wanted to look for her flight number on the blue screen and then find her gate and then sit on those black chairs and wait. I wanted to see her walking out of the gate, arriving. I thought this would slow things down and calm me.

I went alone. Mason had already lost two days of work time; he was late on his promise to deliver the Alfa Romeo. The garage was free tonight and he thought maybe he might be done by seven. Don't worry about it, I said. I could handle it. Besides, I needed some time alone with Nina. Leon hinted about coming with me, but I pretended not to hear him. Last thing I needed was a Leon scene at the airport.

I got there early, half an hour before the flight was due. Since Wednesday, I'd managed to hold off the panic, the fear, but it was always there, a motor whirling the anxiety around like a fan. Finally all the awful details had been set in order. I was grateful that Sergeant Kiernan had given me warning about Ona's body; he recommended other ways for verification, dental charts, fingerprints. Mason said in a fall like that the head sort of explodes. I didn't even have to think about it. I wanted to remember Ona alive, whole. I didn't want to see her broken.

I kept dealing with the outside reality: All the Chinatown funeral houses were shut down because of an old-world fear that it was unlucky to touch death so close to the beginning of a new year. I made arrangements with the crematorium. I talked to all Ona's girlfriends. I told Eddie Jow at The Traders. I fielded the sewing ladies' calls and then their visits. The toughest call was to Osvaldo. It tore me up, hearing him break down. I didn't expect him to be able to make the memorial service.

All the duties had kept me occupied, safe from the true emotion. Now, I began to feel the weight of Ona's death coming toward me, a tiny speck in the distant sky. The oldtimers believe we have a heavenly weight, and that our fates can be divined by the weighing of our bones. But what was left to predict or foresee? Ona was dead.

A rush of feelings rose in me like a fever. Like the morning I first heard about Ona, time went slow and fast and faster and slower, all at once. I walked from gate to gate. I ate candy: M&M's, Reese's, Red Vines, all of it. I skimmed the newspaper headlines: Feinstein and Alioto, the Oakland A's. I stopped and stood by the big windows and watched the sky. A plane shape descended. It was coming closer and closer. I could see it more clearly every second: the wing flaps, the wheels gliding into place. I saw the windows. I saw Ona falling and falling. Any second she was going to land.

I went to the bathroom and splashed my face with cold water. I looked at myself in the mirror: Breathe, I told the haggard face. I touched the fish-belly puffiness under my eyes. My skin was all sallow and patchy and my lips were white. I looked as bad as I felt. The awful news had settled into my face.

I fished in my purse for lipstick, but then I heard Mah's voice: You're not going to a party. I put the lipstick away; I looked at my face. I thought about how I didn't look like anybody, not Mah or Ona or Nina. I used to be jealous of my sisters, how they looked so much like Mah. They had her dark eyes and full lips and the same diamond-shaped face. There was something tropical about their bodies, a warm and easy gracefulness. My sisters were asked all the time if they were twins.

But only one of my sisters was coming off the plane. Seeing Nina would be like seeing Ona. Facing Nina, I'd have to believe Ona was gone.

I thought Nina had missed the flight. It felt like a whole five minutes after the white-haired lady trudged past before I saw Nina turn the bend and walk slowly down the corridor, not looking up till she was right in front of me. She wore dark glasses, which made her look even more pale. Up close, I could see she'd been crying.

Hugging, we held on.

Nina said, "You look awful."

I'd gotten a good look at her while she walked slowly down the corridor, but I didn't mention her flat airplane hair. I gave her an accusing look. "Mah's not going to like what you're wearing."

"What's wrong with it?"

"It's red!"

"Mah loves red."

"Sure, if you're going to a party."

She didn't say anything. It was as if I'd told her she looked like shit.

We walked the whole length of the terminal, rode down the escalator, and walked another corridor, without saying a word to each other. The heavy quiet was like luggage between us. But in my head I was talking to her: What the hell are you thinking? Who do you think you are, breezing off the plane, coming home when all the hard stuff has been taken care of, wearing a totally wrong color, and then getting all bent out of shape when I'm just trying to give you warning?

At the elevators Nina and I stood at attention, facing the doors. I pressed the down button.

"Lei," Nina said, all the edge gone from her voice. I turned and saw that all the defiance was gone from her face, too. "Look," she said, "let's not do this."

What I felt was a miraculous feeling of being saved at the very last minute. I thought, Maybe we've moved that ocean mile forward.

"Yeah," I said. "This is pretty stupid."

She smiled.

I smiled back.

Slow, tentative gestures.

The elevator doors slid open. It was crowded with people and luggage and carts and kids. Nina held the door open until everyone got out, then we stepped in. I pressed the number 4 and the big doors shut. Inside the elevator, the smooth descending momentum made me feel as if I was going way deep down into the vacuum-safe depths of an ocean liner, that we were sailing away.

TWELVE

THE summer Leon found out about Tommie Hom was the worst time. Leon came back from a forty-one-day voyage, the first real work he'd had in over six months, with his pay in his pocket and three stuffed koala bears in his duffel bag. He looked good: tanned and muscled and proud to have money for Mah. But three days later, at Portsmouth Square, he heard about Mah and Tommie. Wives had told their husbands, who told their park-bench buddies, who told the Newspaper Man, who kept on telling till it was old news. So when Jimmy Lowe went up to Leon and said, *"Wey,* Leon, you're wearing a green hat," he thought Leon knew.

When Leon didn't show for dinner—an elaborate vegetarian feast that took Mah days to plan—Ona looked under their bed for his duffel bag. It was gone. We assumed he'd gotten onto a voyage, but we didn't find a goodbye note. Leon always left some kind of note. Once he drew a ship with a stick figure on deck, steering, and all the time he was away, I imagined him as the captain in a peaked hat, not a shirtless laundryman with a towel around his neck. I liked it when he left notes. I liked how he signed his name. I liked how *Leon* almost looked like the twin of *Leong.* His signature reminded me of those nearly symmetrical Chinese characters: door or forest or north.

Most of the time, he left notes in Chinese for Mah. But this time he left nothing, not even his itinerary.

First thing in the morning, I called the Seaman's Union

to ask which ship Leon went out on. Frank Jow barked into my ear, "What do you mean? He's right here, waiting for his number to be called."

That summer, I'd gotten a special permit through Galileo High's summer employment program and they found me a job in the catalog department of the Main Library, so I couldn't go down to the union hall to stop Leon from shipping out. Ona wanted to go. She was only ten, but she knew how to get there; she'd been there with Leon dozens of times.

Ona had no luck. Leon said he was staying at the San Fran until his number came up. When we told Mah, she didn't even take her coat off. The four of us walked down to the San Fran and took the elevator up to the ninth floor. When Leon saw Mah, he spit at her and slammed his hotel door shut. Ona cried and the door swung open again and Leon came out into the hallway and cursed Mah out. Mah started crying but Leon wouldn't stop. Doors opened and old men peered out. Nina hid behind Mah. Ona held Mah's hand and said, "Don't cry." I stood there looking at my shoes. The hallway was dark. It smelled awful. That's what I kept thinking. It felt like forever, us standing there listening to Leon's whole awful story: how he spent his life waiting around at the union halls, how he worked for us and brought home every dollar, how we were ungrateful, and how Mah betrayed him. He said he didn't need us. He said he didn't want Mah.

Ona was determined to show Leon how grateful she was. She wanted to show him how much she needed him. I think Ona probably worked the hardest at getting Leon to come home. Every morning, she went to the San Fran and walked with him to the union hall on Townsend

Street. At first he was embarrassed about having a child following him into the hall, but the men liked Ona. She ran errands for them so that they could hold on to their numbers. The jobbers sent Ona to the corner store for sandwiches and cigarettes or the racing form, and they always told her to buy herself a Coke, some candy. Ona said it was better than staying home. She learned to play poker, blackjack, and American chess. "A television hung like a fan from the ceiling," she told us. When all the jobs were filled, usually before lunch, Leon and Ona ate sandwiches on a bus-stop bench while waiting for the number 21 bus to take them to the employment agencies south of Market Street. Sometimes they made a detour and hunted through the Goodwill Store on Seventeenth Street, or spent the afternoon watching old-style movies at the Grandview Theatre. Ona loved the love stories about the butterfly lovers, fox spirits, snake goddesses, and the four great beauties. Ona told me that when they came out of the theatre the afternoon sun hurt her eyes, made her dizzy.

But most of the time Leon ranted. He cursed his lousy luck: Never a good job, never a good wife. Ona listened. She was patient. Ona had stamina—his stamina—and she'd let him run his steam, and when he was done, she'd work on getting him to come home. It took about a month, but finally he agreed to a meeting. He admitted to Ona that he didn't really like living at the hotel or hanging around the union hall and the Square; he said Croney was a terrible cook. That was why he'd married Mah in the first place.

I don't remember whose idea it was to set the chairs side by side in the kitchen. I do remember the two bare wooden chairs looking like props that I've seen at the Chinese opera.

Mah and Leon sat solemnly, shoulder to shoulder, like a king and queen, and because they weren't facing each other, their furious words fell into their own laps.

Mah pleaded. She cried into her sleeve. She admitted her wrong.

Leon wouldn't look at her; he kept his hands on his knees, his eyes looked straight ahead, down the long corridor, and, I imagined, maybe even out the door.

Mah said, "Everything is in the past." It was over between her and Tommie.

Stoic Leon, sad Leon. He didn't say anything. We could see him working his jaw.

Mah said she wanted to be a family again.

I watched Leon. I saw him nod.

But he didn't move back to Salmon Alley right away. For a week, Mah made him dinner and we took it to him in the same white pot we used for taking meals to Grandpa Leong. Mah began to invite Leon home for special vegetarian dinners. Leon started dropping by to fix things: the fan over the stove, a leaking faucet, a jammed window.

When he signed onto a cargo ship set for Australia, Mah looked for a new job. She thought Leon might move back if she quit Tommie's shop. She couldn't get Tommie completely out of her life because he was our landlord, and Mah couldn't imagine moving away from Salmon Alley. Leon set sail. Mah put the word out that she was looking for another factory. While Leon was still at sea, she heard about an opening at the Ching's, a much larger shop on the Mason-Taylor corner, where the cable cars made their wide turn and changed tracks. Mah loved the lively sound of the brass bells ringing. Mah started as a straight seam seamstress, but by the time Leon returned she had been promoted to the overlock machine.

LEON did move back. A yellow cab brought him straight from the pier. I remember watching Leon lift his duffel bag out of the trunk. He looked good, tanned and smiling and relaxed. He brought us each a beaded coin purse and an alligator handbag for Mah. Friends came by and Leon gave them cubes of what he said was the world's sweetest butter. It was like a big party.

Leon and Mah never talked about Tommie Hom. We all went on trying to be a family, like Mah wanted. But things were never the same. Even their quiet was different. Leon was pensive, sad; Mah's quiet was about being afraid. Any day, I expected to come home and find an itinerary on the table, his duffel bag gone.

I have to give Leon credit, though. During that time, he tried to find steady work on land. One by one, his shipping buddies settled into steady jobs on land. Jimmy Lowe got a janitorial job at the Fairmont Hotel. Croney went to work for relatives who owned the Universal. Cousin went back to cleaning chickens at the chicken store.

Meanwhile, I helped Leon fill out his unemployment forms. *Are you physically able and willing to ship offshore now?*

Check yes, Leon said. But I could tell Leon didn't really like shipping anymore; maybe he wanted to stay home to keep a close eye on Mah, maybe it was true what he said, that he wanted to stay home to see us grow.

Will you "throw in" for every job your shipping card permits you to take?

Yes.

During the next couple of years, Leon shipped just enough to keep his card valid. Between voyages, he worked odd jobs in the hopes of finding something good enough to let his card go. He was the fry cook at Wa-jin's, the barbecue chef at Golden Dragon, a janitor in the financial district, a busboy, the night porter at The Oasis. He took a welding class and then worked the graveyard shift with Bethlehem Steel in Alameda.

All the while, Leon kept his eye open for new opportunities. He and Jimmy Lowe put in a bid for a takeout place in Vallejo. They even had a name for it: The Phoenix Walk-Away. I don't know why it didn't work out. Who knows how many more? All I know is that after Mah let Leon talk her into trying to make a go of the grocery store—while still holding on to her job at the shop—she never wanted to go into business with him again.

L. L. Grocery was on Pacific Avenue, near Powell, across from the Mobil station. Leon opened the store in the mornings while Mah sewed at the factory; Mah watched the store from four to nine, while Leon worked his graveyard shift at the steelyard. We practically lived at the grocery. I remember after school and weekends there: dusting the shelves and stocking canned goods and taking trips to the wholesaler on Stockton for paper supplies. We helped count loaves of Kilpatrick's bread as they were delivered. We rotated the milk in the refrigerator; I remember Borden's milk with the cow named Elsie. We kept the aisles stacked with salted fish and preserved turnips and dried red dates. Nina liked the baseball cards and cotton candy and crackerjack. Ona liked to watch the bubble-gum man count out his pennies in the back room, and she believed him when he said he'd make gumballs out of her if she broke another one of his glass fixtures.

We helped watch the store for the hour and a half between English School's letting out and Chinese School's beginning; it was enough time for Mah to do the dinner shopping. After Chinese School, we sat at the counter by the register doing our homework while Mah cooked dinner in the back room.

It wouldn't have been so bad if the store had made a profit. But business was bad. Food went stale on the shelves. Salesmen cheated Leon, smooth-talked Mah. Kids stole candy and cigarettes. I sneaked baseball cards to the boys I liked. Our only steady customers were oldtimers who came by and sat on a stool by the door and read the newspaper for free. Every week, half of Leon's Bethlehem check went into the store. When I was finishing junior high, Leon sold the L. L. Grocery at a loss.

That winter, Bethlehem Steel relocated and Leon got laid off. One wild scheme followed another. Cousin told him about a bankrupt noodle factory in Sacramento. They decided to buy the machinery and dismantle it and haul it down to San Francisco to sell, but when they tried to put it back together, crucial parts had mysteriously disappeared and they ended up selling it all for scrap.

He had better luck with the coffee. When prices soared, Jimmy Lowe told Leon that he had a friend who had a friend who was looking to sell several hundred sacks of beans. Leon bought them all and went into business supplying the Chinatown pastry shops with discount coffee. He stored the sacks under the stairway and the aroma filled the apartment for a year. Once in a while, I still catch a whiff of it as I walk up the steps.

Too much dreaming, Mah said of Leon's big-money talk. But she'd lived with him long enough to understand his need to wander, to be lost in new places, new things. She shook her head, exasperated, but I don't think she ever gave up hope. She told us for a man with so many failures, Leon had a heart full of hope. Each new scheme, each voyage was his way of showing us his heart.

But Mah grew weary of Leon's schemes. She tried out her idea on me first. What if they went into business together, she and Leon? Full time. Outside Chinatown. What if they really put all their effort into something? She wanted Leon to quit shipping. She said she was ready to quit the sewing shops. I was glad to hear it. I'd watched the years of working in the sweatshops change her body. Her neck softened. Her shoulders grew heavy. Work was her whole life, and every forward stitch marked time passing. She wanted to get out before her whole life passed under the stamping needle.

When I was younger, I hated to hear Mah's confidential tone. Her words fell on me like a heavy weight. I took her questions seriously, as though it were really my choice. When I was five years old, she asked me who I preferred, Tommie Hom or Leon Leong. First, I thought to say Tommie, because something about him reminded me of the way Mah talked about my father, but I said Leon, because he brought me presents and because I knew he went out to sea. I didn't want anybody to come between me and Mah. Tommie owned most of Salmon Alley. He was always coming and going with his gangster buddies.

But over the years of listening, I learned that Mah was just lonely. All she wanted was someone to talk to. I learned to listen until I knew what she wanted, and then to tell her what she needed to hear. Maybe that's what I always did. Maybe I knew she wanted Leon more than Tommie.

Quit, I told her. Get out of the shops.

Mah also talked to Rosa Ong, who sewed beside her at Tommie's. We'd known the Ongs since they first came from Peru. They lived in an old Victorian apartment building on the corner of Jones and Pacific, which was only a couple blocks from Salmon Alley, but as far as we were concerned, that was outside Chinatown. When Rosa walked into the shop, she could barely thread the Singer, but Tommie hired her anyway and assigned Mah the job of teaching her to sew. The usual gossip started going around: Tommie had hired another pretty, know-nothing seamstress. The other ladies didn't trust Rosa because she was half Spanish, but Mah liked her pretty eyes and lilting accent, and she taught Rosa all her secret tricks to fool Tommie: what he looked for when he inspected their work (zippers), what he never looked at (darts, the hem). And when she called us to come to the factory to iron interfacing or turn sashes, she told us to do Rosa's, too.

Mah and Rosa were like sisters. They joked that they sewed more than they slept, and sewing side by side, they were more intimate with each other than with their husbands. They had subtle rivalries. Mah envied Rosa her sunny apartment outside Chinatown, her creamy complexion, her long lashes, her musical laugh, but most of all, Mah envied her her sons, Aurelio and Osvaldo. Rosa wished she could sew as fast as Mah. She wished she could look at the sample pattern and know all the secret seams that filled out a dress. She envied Mah her slender brow, her small feet. She wished Tommie liked her as much as he seemed to like Mah. (Rosa, being a newcomer, was outside the circle of gossip and she didn't know the whole story about Mah and Tommie.) But mostly Rosa wished she had a daughter.

She visited us often on Salmon Alley. She and Mah

stayed up late copying dress patterns, talking about Miss Tsai, making festival food. Rosa taught us how to crochet and made each of us a lace shawl; we called her Auntie.

Even though they lived only three blocks away, Rosa's husband, Luciano, always picked her up in his big black Monte Carlo, a ship on narrow Salmon Alley. The gossip was that he bought it with cash. The ladies all had something to say. Impossible to park. Where'd he get the money? Does he think he's such a big shot in a black car?

Luciano Ong blew into Chinatown like a thunderstorm. We loved looking at him in his embroidered shirts, his Sun Yat-sen mustache. Nina liked his Ricky Ricardo hair style. Big-boned, broad-backed, and loud-voiced, he was the tallest man in Portsmouth Square. A crowd always gathered around him to hear about his next big idea. He always had a plan to make big money, but he always seemed to need one more grand. He was always one man short.

Luciano was Leon's kind of guy. Leon called Luciano *Dai Gor*, Big Brother. He tried to impress him with all the Spanish words he'd learned on the ships: *muchacha, maricón, calle, merengue*. He boasted about having been to South America himself, Rio de Janeiro and Santiago and Cape Horn, even to the Chinatown in Lima. Hadn't he given his last daughter a Spanish name, in honor of Columbus's fleet? (Nina was horrified.) Leon wanted to be Luciano's last man; he wanted to have the honor of giving him the grand that would make his big-money dreams come true.

Leon talked about Luc all the time. Every story he heard Luc tell at the Square he repeated for us at dinner. Luc tipped Paul Lim twenty dollars for parking his car. Luc bought snakeskin shoes at Florsheim. Luc had a gold Rolex. Soon Luc was going to buy a new Cadillac.

One night Mah accused Leon of being jealous of Luc,

but Leon insisted that he wasn't. He didn't want the things Luc had, he wanted Luc's secret to success, his good fortune. That's when Mah talked to Leon about wanting to leave the sewing shop. She told him that she had been talking with Rosa about her own plans of finding a business outside Chinatown. She gave Leon the go-ahead to talk to Luc about a partnership.

The next day, he approached Luc with a proposition: fifty-fifty. Ong and Leong. Luciano liked the sound of that. Their names fit together like a pair of chopsticks that they could eat with for the rest of their lives. For weeks, they met at the Universal to read the classified ads in *The Chinese Times*, *The Chronicle*, and *The Examiner*. Luciano drove Leon around the city in his fancy car to look at shoe-repair shops and restaurants and a bowling alley at West Lake shopping mall. They sat in the projection booth of the Great World Movie Palace trying to bargain the price of the palace down. They negotiated with the Fong Brothers as the big machines churned out tubs of ice cream; they learned to work a photo-developing machine somewhere in the Marina.

I never saw Leon happier. Every morning he got up early and put on his double-breasted blue suit and his luck-red tie. He polished his shoes until they shone almost as brightly as Luc's. Before the sewing ladies arrived for work, Leon was at the front of the alley, waiting for Luciano.

The day they decided on the laundry, Leon came home with a whole duck and a pound of roast pork, Mah's favorites, and a strawberry cake, our favorite. In the morning, Mah withdrew their savings from the bank.

THE Ong & Leong laundry was on McAllister Street, on the seedy edge of the Tenderloin. To get there, we took

the number 30 Stockton bus downtown and then trans-
ferred to the 38 Geary and got off on Polk and walked two
blocks past massage parlors and all-male strip joints and
the Mitchell Brothers' famous theatre. The storefront had
two small rooms: in front there was a long wooden counter
worn smooth from use and an ancient cash register, a relic
from the days when the place was a retail laundry, in back,
a storage room and a kitchenette where Mah made lunch.
A narrow staircase led to a basement that was as wide and
as deep as the belly of a ship. The first time I went down
there, I stood at the bottom of the stairs and watched Leon
navigate through the gloom. One by one, he found the
overhanging bulbs and pulled their strings and sent the
lights swinging over each dusty machine.

Leon taught us how to twist the sheets like rope, so they
wouldn't knot up while washing, and how to lift them out
of the machine without straining our backs. We used both
arms to carry them to the extractor, a wild spinning contraption that whined like Dr. Joe's drill. We learned to
work the press, a two-girl job. Ona and I held opposite
corners of the damp sheet and slipped the edges under the
hot rollers. After the edges caught, we ran around to the
other end where the sheet slid out, stiff and hot and dry.
We folded them by the hotel-loads, corner touching corner, until each package was as tight and perfect as a new
deck of cards.

It was hot down there. The humid air was chalky with
starch and soap and bleach. The steam and chlorine odor
clung to us. Once I smelled it on myself and was surprised
with the clear memory of Leon coming home.

That summer, we were all on call for helping out at the
laundry, which was almost all the time. I was taking education classes at San Francisco State University and working

full time as a receptionist in the campus Career Center. Ona took classes at City College and worked the five-to-ten evening shift at Chinatown Bazaar. Nina'd just graduated from Galileo High and hadn't decided what she wanted to do yet, so she clocked in the most hours at the laundry and hated every minute of it. She said the only good thing about lifting the wet sheets was that her arms looked good in a tank top.

For Ona, Osvaldo was the best thing about Ong & Leong's. I remember watching him once. He carried two fifty-pound sacks of laundry out to the van and he tossed them through the open door as if they were goose-down pillows. He had Luc's broad back and Rosa's golden skin. Her Spanish blood gave him the dark lashes and strong jaw of a pretty-boy actor. Ona said Osvaldo looked even better than Fu Sheng, her favorite *gung fu* hero.

Soon she could time his deliveries. Somehow she could sense his presence upstairs. It was as though she could hear his footsteps above her, over the rumble of the washers. Then she wanted a Coke, or had to make a phone call or go to the bathroom or tell Mah something urgent. She'd stay up there for a half hour at a time—sometimes longer—talking to Osvaldo. When Nina complained that Ona wasn't doing her share, Mah surprised us by saying, "Let her have her fun." Leon let Ona go on deliveries with Osvaldo when it was slow. He called her Osvaldo's assistant. When there was a rush order and they needed Ona to work that extra forty minutes it would have taken her to commute to her job, Leon asked Osvaldo to drive Ona to Chinatown Bazaar.

No one was surprised to see them together upstairs, sitting on top of a pile of laundry bags and holding hands.

Mah made only one rule. She asked Ona to please not sit on his lap in the front of the store where anyone walking by could see. Ona did it anyway, but as a gesture to respect Mah's wishes, she pushed the big rubber plant in front of the window. Leon started calling Osvaldo "son," and Mah and Rosa giggled about being sisters.

Ong & Leong inherited the previous owners' hotel clientele, but Luc took it on himself to drum up more business. He called himself the marketing manager, the outside man. He called Leon the plant manager. Leon was the inside man in charge of the whole washing operation. Mah told Leon to go with Luc to the hotels once in a while to learn the business end of things, which was her way of telling him to keep an eye on Luc, but Leon said he was too busy. Luc was the talker and Leon was the worker. Leon claimed he liked it that way.

When there was a lull, Ona and Nina and I always ran upstairs to sit in the light by the big front window. But not Leon. He liked it down there with his machines. The sound of all the washers going, the extractors spinning, the dryers hissing calmed him. Mah said it was as if he was in the engine room of his own ship. She took his dinner down to him, a big soup bowl piled high with rice and vegetables, and he'd walk around, his bowl balanced in his palm, listening to his machines. He knew every machine by its sound. He said that each motor had a different voice, and he could tell when one was getting tired, ready to break down.

All summer, one by one, they all did break down. Leon always got them working again somehow, but we worried, especially Mah. Would the dryers be hot enough? Would the extractors spin? Would we make the deadline?

THEN Ong & Leong's went bust. We had no warning. Luc kept the books; we never saw the summonses or the eviction notices or the unpaid utility bills. We found out one rainy Saturday morning in late November when we arrived and found the place padlocked shut. None of our keys worked. I held an umbrella over Leon as he called Luc from the corner phone booth, but there was no answer. Leon slammed the phone down so hard he cracked the earpiece.

We knew not to ask anything right then. I knew the money was gone. Leon and Luc had only shaken hands on the deal. There was no contract, no legal partnership. I blamed myself. I should have done more; I should have made them go to a lawyer to set the business up. But I hadn't. Mah and Leon seemed so high on the idea, I didn't want to bring in doubt. It was their business, and if they wanted to do things the Chinatown way, if they wanted to depend on old-world trust, I didn't think it was my place to interfere.

Leon went looking for Luc, which was also the old-world way. He didn't show for dinner. Midnight. Still no Leon. We didn't say what we were all afraid of. Ona wanted to call Osvaldo, but Mah wouldn't let her. We sat together in the living room. We waited until two o'clock and then Mah told us to go to bed.

I lay in bed, trying not to fall asleep.

Mah's hoarse voice scared me awake. "Why did it come to this? How could it come to this?"

We knew to stay in our rooms. We listened and the footsteps told us enough: Mah's slippers slapping from bathroom to kitchen to bedroom and Leon's heavy boots dragging down the hall. Their bedroom door shut and then we could only catch the high and low pitches of sound changing: screams and low groans and then a steady silence.

Leon stayed in his room for two days. Mah brought him his meals. She wanted to call a doctor, but Leon said, No. Mah went and found Rosa and flew into a fury. Rosa played innocent: she had no idea; she had no power over her husband, no knowledge of the details. So Mah fumed at us.

I told her, "Don't think about it. It's over now."

Trust, the old-world way. We hadn't been paid for the five months of work we'd put in, and all our savings were gone. I asked for a month's advance pay from my job. Ona was paid in cash every Friday. Mah asked Mr. Ching for her old job, but he'd already hired another seamstress, so Mah went back to Tommie's.

We didn't talk about Leon's bruised and swollen face or his limp. We left him alone and soon his sullenness spread through the apartment. Maybe our quiet was a way to express our own fear and sense of disbelief, of defeat. I'd had my own dreams for the laundry, that a successful business would bring Mah and Leon back together in a deeper way. Around then, a letter came from my father, wanting to make contact, a long-lost, rekindling letter, but there was too much happening for me to feel anything for someone as far away as Australia. I was getting close to Mason and I wanted my own life. I didn't want to worry about Mah or Leon or anybody else.

Ona worried me in a way I couldn't let go of. I always felt that she had the most to lose. She was too sensitive, too close to Leon. When she was little, she'd be weepy for days after Leon left on a voyage, and she'd wait for him, shadowy and pensive, counting off the days till he came home. Every time he lost a job, she went into a depression with him. When he got high on some scheme, she was drunk on it, too. Mah said she was like Leon that way: Ona had no skin.

I think Nina had the best attitude. Leon's problems were his and Mah's were hers, and she hated Chinatown and she was getting out.

Leon started coming and going at strange hours. He spent his days at the park, or with his buddies at the Universal or the Jackson Cafe. Evenings, he wandered around Waverly Place, visiting the chess clubs. He'd come home way after midnight, and then he always cooked up a snack. It confused my dreams to smell rice steaming with salted fish.

When Mah tried to talk to him, he turned on her, blaming her for everything. "Your fault. Women's talk, sewing-lady gossip."

I should have seen it coming: Leon turned on Ona, too. He told her to break up with Osvaldo. "I forbid you to see that mongrel boy. Crooked father, crooked son."

Nina told Ona, "Just say whatever Leon needs to hear. Then you can do whatever you want." I agreed but Ona refused to lie. She told Leon she loved Osvaldo.

Leon threatened to disown her. "You will no longer be my daughter, I will no longer be your father."

What did he think, this was like a divorce? Just because he said something it would be true? But in a strange way, after those words came out of his mouth, it was all over. Forbidding Ona was like daring her.

Leon was relentless. His frustration went deeper than losing the laundry. He blamed himself for the humiliation.

And every time he saw Osvaldo, he remembered his whole past, every job he got fired from, every business that failed. He hung up on Osvaldo, refused to let him into the house. He yelled at Ona every night all through dinner. The harder Leon pressed, the tighter Ona and Osvaldo became.

Once Leon blocked her at the door. He said, "I'm warning you! If you go, don't bother coming back!"

That night, Leon did lock her out. So Ona spent the night at Osvaldo's. Maybe that's when she started to keep secrets. Maybe she figured the less any of us knew, the better.

Then the Ongs moved out to the Richmond district and Ona spent even more time there. We hardly saw her. I heard that it was Luc who put in the call that got Ona her job at The Traders.

I worried about her. Not only because she was Leon's target, but also because she didn't have an out.

The thing that stuck in my mind was what Ona told me about how she felt outside Chinatown. She never felt comfortable, even with the Chinese crowd that Osvaldo hung around with; she never felt like she fit in.

My out was Mason. Nina had a part-time job at Kentucky Fried Chicken on Bay, near Tower Records.

Mah told Leon that Ona would outgrow Osvaldo. I tried talking to him; Nina did, too. We even got Cousin to tell him to let up on Ona, but Leon turned on everyone. I started hoping that Leon would ship out: I thought a voyage might clear his head.

At work one day, I took a job call for a dishwasher at the University of San Francisco Medical Center. I took a chance and sent Leon. I figured, How can he fuck up a dishwashing interview?

But in my desperation to get Leon out of the house I

didn't even consider the obvious—they'd called a student employment office, they'd expect a student.

Leon came home in a rage. "They asked if I had experience!" He fumed, "Who doesn't have experience washing dishes?"

But they offered Leon the job and it seemed to give him some balance. It calmed him, but I knew that would pass.

THE night everything finally blew up, I realized it had been inevitable, but all week I'd been too tired to see the warning signs. Ona had been with Osvaldo for three nights. Leon had some problem with his supervisor. I was beat from work and beat from staying out late with Mason. I came home glad that dinner was ready; all I wanted to do was eat and then go to bed. Leon came in just as we finished eating. Mah had put some dinner aside for him. She went to heat it up.

Then there was a knock and Ona was going down the hall and it was Osvaldo standing there, Osvaldo bending forward, Osvaldo kissing Ona.

It happened fast: Leon getting up and going down the hall after Ona. Ona rushing out the door and Leon following her. Then I ran after them and Mah's scared voice was behind me, asking, "What's happening? What's happening?"

I stopped at the top of the stairs. I saw Leon yank the car door open and reach in, grabbing at Ona. Doors opened up and down the alley. Lights came on.

But Ona kept fighting him. She pushed and flung her arms, she hit him. Leon was yelling something in Chinese, but I couldn't make out what. Mah started yelling, too; she tried to rush down, but I blocked her and told her, "No!" I didn't want her hysteria to feed his.

Ona's screams filled the entire alley.

Osvaldo yelled, "Leave her alone!"

But Leon wouldn't acknowledge Osvaldo. He kept yelling at Ona, "You better listen to me, I'm warning you, if you want to be my daughter, you better listen."

"Leave her alone," Osvaldo shouted again. He got into the car; the engine turned over.

From the top of the stairs, I saw the neighbors back away from their windows, turn off their lights, shut their doors. The alley darkened, became very still. I could barely make out Leon's shadow. Then Osvaldo's headlights flashed on and flooded the alley for a second before sweeping away onto Pacific Avenue. It was only one swift moment of light, but it lasted long enough for me to see Leon looking after Ona as if he was watching everything he'd ever hoped for disappear.

THIRTEEN

THERE was a time when Salmon Alley was our whole world and we all got along. Leon pronounced it *"get long,"* and there was something about the way the English words came out—slow and solid—almost like his voice was building something. It was as if he were talking about one of the Confucian virtues: loyalty or filial piety or sacred ceremony. *"To get long"* meant to make do, to make well of whatever we had; it was about having a long view, which was endurance, and a long heart, which was hope. Mah and Leon, Nina and Ona and I, we all had a lot of hope, those early years on Salmon Alley.

Late August, the Thursday before Labor Day weekend, before school began, the day the S.S. *Independent* was docking: Leon was coming home. I'd rushed all morning to clean the house and help Mah sew a dozen culottes. I finished just before noon. I heated up yesterday's pot of rice, the last of the salted fish, steamed a vegetable, and set the bowls out for Ona and Nina. Then I carried Mah's lunch and the two bundles of culottes to Tommie's.

Ona and Nina were standing at the mouth of the alley, waiting for Leon's cab. They were wearing the I Love Lucy dresses Mah stayed up late to finish. I told them lunch was ready, and they ran down the alley, their full skirts flouncing up and down.

Walking into the factory felt like walking into the cable-car barn. Every machine was running at high speed: the Singers zoomed, the button machines clicked. The shop vibrated like a big engine. Everything blended: oil and metal and the eye-stinging heat of the presses. The ladies pushed their endurance, long hours and then longer nights, as they strained to slip one more seam under the stamping needle.

The sewing ladies called them skirt-pants and Mah promised me a pair for the first day of school. It was an easy pattern: four darts, four straight seams, and a simple zipper. Six dollars per dozen. Mah could finish a dozen in a little over an hour (Miss Tsai took at least two). A pattern like this came around once a season, and every shop in Chinatown was rushing its orders. On Stockton Street, ladies stopped their rivals from other shops and compared wages. Every lady smiled, every lady nodded: This pattern was easier than eating rice. All the ladies were working overtime at the shop. Mah even had Tommie deliver bundles to our apartment, and I helped sew them on our Singer.

The pattern before had been a different story: a linen shift with a row of buttons like five pairs of fingernails, from the neckline down to the knees. The ladies complained about the lining, that it was like sewing two dresses for the price of one. Tommie was a nervous wreck. He was late on his order, but the ladies paid him no mind; languid and slow, they took long tea breaks and cracked melon seeds delicately between their teeth. They turned the tape machines up so high I could hear the cymbals and bugles and gongs and the shrieking of the Cantonese opera from down the alley. Tommie, desperate, disconnected the speaker system, but the ladies brought in their own radios and cassette players, and he had to yell out the deadlines over the bells. Still, the ladies laughed, screeching along with the opera cat voices.

With the culotte pattern, the opera was never even

turned on, because the ladies were as competitive as gamblers and only wanted to listen to each other zooming along.

Mah was too busy even to look up when I offered her her lunch. She said she didn't have an appetite, so I put the aluminum packet of food on the water pipe, where it'd stay warm, and her thermos on the already-filled communal eating table.

She wanted to teach me to do zippers so I could sew another dozen for her at home. Mah's zippers were as flat and smooth as her seams. Speed was essential, but I could barely follow Mah's hands. She spun the dress pieces, and the needle was a blur, churning alongside the tracks of the zipper. The blue spool rippled over her head.

Mah knew all the seams of a dress the way a doctor knows bones. She went quickly through the other parts: how to sew the darts, which she called *"the folds,"* when to sew all the connecting seams, called *"the big bones,"* and the special seams for the hems of each skirt, *"the feet."*

My head was twirling, but I nodded again.

Mah asked if I'd called the union to check on Leon's ship. I told her what Frank Jow told me, that the crew wasn't allowed off till after six. "Come get me when he gets here," she said.

I picked up the huge stuffed bags and started to leave. Overhead, the dusty fans whirled, but I didn't feel much of a breeze. My bags tapped against Miss Tsai's chair accidentally. She looked up and made a huumph face at me, then grumbled, "Some people are lucky, having so many daughters to help out."

I bumped her, this time on purpose, and then left.

Ona and Nina were jumping rope in the alley. I warned

them that Leon wouldn't get home till dark, but they wanted to wait.

Back home, I started with the darts. I sewed the facing to the interfacing, the front to the back; then I had trouble with the zipper. I wasn't used to the slick gabardine fabric; my seams didn't match up, and the needle kept sliding over to the metal teeth. I undid the seam and tried again. This time the needle hit the metal zipper tab and jammed. I gave up, afraid I might break the needle. Mah broke a needle once and its tip flew up and lodged so close to her eye that Luday and Soon-ping had to walk her over to Chinese Hospital.

I was taking the crooked stitches out when Ona came in, yelling, "He's here! He's here!" Then, quick and relieved, she added, "He looks just the same."

Ona had worried that Leon might come back a different man, with a bigger nose, maybe a foreigner. I always thought that Leon came back more relaxed, a new man. I loved how he tanned, a dark sugar tone that made his white shirt glow, and I loved the way he smelled like the sea.

Downstairs, the yellow cab was backed into the alley, its trunk open. Leon pulled his duffel bag out of the trunk and paid the driver. Ona and Nina were dragging a huge laundry sack out of the backseat. I ran down the alley to get Mah.

That first night, Mah cooked an elaborate meal of all Leon's favorites: crunchy pig-ear appetizers, tripe, sea cucumbers sautéed in black mushrooms, dried bean curd, fatty pork, stewed duck, many vegetables. We watched Leon wolf his dinner down. His chopsticks reached out again and again, snapping, clicking. When Leon was home, we never ate leftovers.

Mah explained that it was from lack. "Out at sea for forty-one days."

AFTER dinner, Mah brought out a stack of newspapers she'd saved for Leon. "This will keep you busy," she said. Then she went to the front room to finish the culottes. He took the pile and smiled his big smile at her, but he didn't read them right away. He walked around the apartment, taking an inventory of everything that had broken down.

When Leon was away, we let things go. A jammed door remained shut, a leaking faucet wasn't used. We piled on sweaters when the radiator was broken. One night's leftovers became the next day's breakfast: a salted fish cut into slivers, steamed in oil, and seasoned with ginger slices.

While I washed the dishes, Ona swept the kitchen and Nina cleared and wiped off the kitchen table. Then Leon went to his S.S. *Independent* laundry bag and took out the paper bag he always used for his cash pay. He held the old bag on his open palm as if he were weighing it. Leon's ritual. He wanted us to see every dollar he made.

I spread the bills out in a fan and waved; they crackled and smelled like the ground ink that we used in Chinese school. I started the stacks: ones, fives, tens, and twenties.

Nina fingered each stack and said, "We're rich!"

"So much money," Ona said quietly.

Leon smiled. "Overtime."

I counted each stack twice. And then I went into the other room to tell Mah how much. She smiled but didn't look up from the zippers she was working on.

LATE that night, I heard Mah and Leon talking in the bedroom.

"Not enough," Mah said.

Her voice was steady, but I couldn't make out the items she listed. I imagined Mah counting, each finger naming a debt, her hand tightening into a fist.

I saw the fist. Two hands praying. Two fists sparring.

Then I heard Leon's low, deep voice. "It's as much as I could. You don't know. You're inside Chinatown; it's safe. You don't know. Outside, it's different."

I heard low sounds and then nothing. I imagined their blanket pulled tightly around them.

Out at sea, I knew that Leon hardly slept. He worked double shifts—one night slipped into another, tied together by a few hours' sleep. He told me it wasn't time he was spending, it was sweat. He said life was work and death the dream.

When I heard Mah again, her voice was softer. "You have to go back."

WAITING to fall asleep, I listened to the tick-ah-tock, tick-ah-tock of minutes passing, one hour ending and another beginning, everything adding up.

Somehow, I knew it would be the same as always. Leon would go back, ship out on the next voyage, sail away. We'd wait for him again. Tomorrow and tomorrow would be the same. Night after night, we'd eat from the salted fish, from the silver tail on up to the yellowed head, until forty-one slivers of salted fish later Leon would come back home again.

FOURTEEN

MAH left early to get her hair electrified at Duckie's Mom's. On her way out, she tapped on my door. "Get up, Leila!" she said. "Leon's coming home today. Clear a space in the bathroom. And vacuum! Don't forget under the couch." The door clicked shut. Like the journeys of the eight holy immortals, Leon's comings and goings ordered Mah's life.

Mah thought his work as a merchant seaman was a good thing, because it kept him away for months at a time. She had learned from experience: my father was a wolf; he married her quickly and just as quickly he left her. Now she thought it was better to let a man into her life slowly.

She married Leon for the green card. It was no secret; even Leon knew that was why she said yes. He didn't care; he knew his card was good forever.

This voyage was special; the S.S. *Independent* was docking two days in Melbourne, and Leon planned to look up the father I've never seen, Lyman Fu. This time I was as nervous as Mah about Leon's return.

Mason and I were still in bed. I listened to Mah's footsteps going down the rickety steps, then rolled over and hugged Mason; there was a faint metal smell in his hair.

"Huh?" Mason stirred. "What?"

"She just gave me a list of things to do, getting-ready-for-Leon stuff." Then I whispered, ". . . and she said not to sleep the morning away with you."

"Nah." He gave a laugh. "She likes me now. I can tell."

In the beginning, Mah didn't like Mason's staying over, so I made him leave in the middle of the night. He was working on the Karmann Ghia then, and it made such a racket starting up that Mah finally gave in. She said, "Better for the neighbors to see the car in the morning and wonder than for them to look out the window in the middle of the night and know."

The first time Mason came over, I waited for him downstairs. It was night and the street lamp on Pacific poured a sliver of light into Salmon Alley. His white car glistened, clean as the inside of a cut turnip.

There's an old blue sign at the bottom of our steps: #2—4—6 UPDAIRE. You can't miss it and it was the first thing Mason saw. He pointed at the sign with his chin. Then he threw his head back and laughed.

"D-A-I-R-E?" He looked at me and laughed again.

I shrugged. So? I thought. It was my address; it was home, where I lived.

Mason is a little strange about having been born and raised in Chinatown; sometimes he's proud and sometimes he's not. Most of my other boyfriends didn't feel comfortable outside of Chinatown; they didn't even much like doing things outside the family. Mason likes to ski and he goes to Tahoe as much as he can. He doesn't care if he's the only Chinese guy on the expert runs; he knows he's good enough. What surprises me is that he never gambles. "It's too Chinesey," he says. There's that about him, though; sometimes he says things in that half-embarrassed tone.

When we were getting to know each other, I liked that we did things on our own, so I didn't ask about his family.

But then I started to wonder: Didn't they care about him? Didn't he like me enough to introduce me to them?

I asked around and my friend Patricia Woo told me what she heard. "Real messed-up family, his sister married a white guy, and a brother overdosed."

"Hey," Mason said now, nudging me. "Looks like she's in a good mood today, maybe you could tell her, huh?"

Mason was moving into his own place in the Mission, and he wanted me to move in with him. I wanted to, but I didn't know how Mah would take it.

"Maybe," I said. I didn't know how to tell her. One thing I liked about Mason: he *said* things. I mean, I thought about a lot of things, but I never actually *said* them. Out loud. I turned away from him, gave a kick under the covers to show my irritation.

"Just don't take too long, is all I'm saying," he said.

I knew why I was putting it off; I was waiting for Leon, too. I expected him to bring back something from this meeting with my father—a word, a picture, an expression—something that would unlock me from Mah, this alley, Chinatown.

"I can't help it, I just feel like I owe her. It's always been just me and her."

Mason's voice was soft. "Lei, she's got Leon."

I REMEMBER when Mah first told me about Leon. I was six and Mah took me out for dim sum lunch to tell me she was going to marry him.

"He'll make a suitable husband," she said. "One, he's got his papers; two, he works at sea. He'll be away a lot. It'll be just you and me. Like now. I won't have to work so hard, we can take it a little easier."

"Fuun! Fuun! Shrimp, pork, beef!" The waitress called out the items on her cart in a bored singsong. Mah waved to her and asked for a plate of shrimp and beef.

I wasn't surprised about Leon Leong. I knew Mah was looking for a husband. Mr. Yee, the presser at the factory, brought her breakfast sweets. There was Mr. Wing, the day manager at Silver Palace, and Tony Owyang, with his own electronics company. After Leon, Mah liked her boss, Tommie, second best—he was a spender, but not a talker. Money is a good thing, Mah said, but so is a pretty mouth and a heady compliment.

"Why him?" I said.

"He asked me." Mah cut a piece of *fuun* with her chopsticks. "What do you think?"

I poured soy over my *fuun*, swirled it around on my plate, then put the whole sloppy piece in my mouth. I'd seen Leon only a few times, so I didn't know what to say. I chewed. "Well," I said, "he's kinda bald up there."

Mah laughed. "You know the saying, 'Ten bald men and nine are rich.' "

Mah and Leon were married in Reno. I was their witness. Leon's cousin was service manager at Harrah's and booked The Pink Room at a discount. Mah finished our dresses the night before. Pink lace over pink satin, a princess neckline, cap sleeves, an empire waist, and a big satin bow in the back.

I coached Mah about the ceremony. "The man'll look up at you after saying a lot of stuff. Just say, 'I do.' And nod." But when she said it in the justice's office, her accent made it sound like a question. "I do?"

Afterwards, we gambled. Mah and I played the slot machines in between watching Leon play poker. Two busloads from Chinatown arrived bringing some of Mah's sewing-lady friends. They had coupons for free coffee and they invited Mah, so I walked around the mall and looked into the shops. I was fingering a suede shoulder bag when Leon came up from behind.

"Do you want it?" he asked.

This is what I'd worried about all through the bus ride up here: what to call him after they married. I expected Mah to give me instructions, but she didn't, and now Leon and I were alone. I just stared at the bag.

"Let me buy it," he said.

I shrugged. I drew my finger back and forth on the suede, making lines.

He handed me two twenties and nodded toward the register. "Go on." He smiled. "Pay the lady. It's a souvenir."

When we stepped out of the store, I turned and said thanks, but avoided looking at him.

"No need." He tapped my shoulder lightly, like he was saying thanks.

The leather smell was strong. I looked at the bag and wondered if the braided straps and long suede fringe were me. Would I ever use this? Was it too American? I worried that I was wasting his money. I looked straight at him, and asked, "What do I call you now?"

He shrugged. "Call me Leon . . . or call me 'L.' That's what they call me on the ships."

Lyman Fu, my real father, was called many things. In the villages, he was known as the Fa-fa Prince, a garden stroller, a flower picker.

Mah said, "In those days, we didn't have a choice. I was young and he picked me."

Mah said he told her, "I don't need a matchmaker; I don't need a pointer or a list. I could have picked you blind. You don't belong on these muddy roads, in these water-carrying villages. Come with me, let's go! To fast, fast Hong Kong."

"A few good years," Mah said, ". . . ate well, dressed well. There was a motorcar."

"But like a blink," Mah cried, "he lost it all, lost it fast, slapping tiles on a three-night mah-jongg run."

After that, she called him *Talk Big Words*. He took his stories about gold and the easy life down to the docks, into the bars, the gambling dens and whorehouses. The lame ones, the beardless boys, the gamblers; they all listened. Lyman Fu encouraged the dreamers. He was a crimp, a coolie broker.

He had plans. America, the big gold mountain, was where he wanted to settle. They came to San Francisco together but things didn't work out as fast as he wanted. Then he heard that Australia was the new gold mountain, every coolie's dream.

"A few years is all I need," he promised. "I'll send for you," he said.

Mah believed; she thought the child growing in her belly was insurance.

But I wasn't a son and no tickets came in the mail.

Every spring Mah sent him my picture to remind him: *This daughter is yours, this daughter is growing.* She cut my hair, bought me a new dress, and told me to smile for him.

I've never seen him. When I say "never seen," I'm thinking of the Chinese term, "seen his face." I've seen his picture and read his letters. I know him by the name he used in letters. "Your father, Fu Lyman."

As a child, I traced over his characters: *Are you my good daughter? Would you make me proud?*

Mah saved all his letters and studied them, turned his

phrases inside out. She read them out loud and asked, "What does it sound like to you? Does he want to come back?"

I grew up waiting on the mail, too, collecting stamps; Australia was the biggest part of my collection. I held the miniature pictures in my palm: the big rock, the koalas, Queen Elizabeth. The scalloped edges pieced together the faint world he lived in, but the more I had, the more of him I felt I owned.

His money orders shrank first in figures and then in frequency, until Mah said they were only eggs, rotten ones.

In his last letter, his message fit into one square corner. Each stroke was bold, magnified: *Leila, Don't blame me.*

Mah's eyes dimmed from crying and then from anger. She was inconsolable. She went to bed with questions: "Tell me *how* to live? *How* to face life? *How* to see people?" She woke with curses: "Turtle! Salted egg! Drunk head!"

Mah ran out into the alley, shouting into the black night: "Ai! Ai! Aiyah!!" Her cries told the whole story: the runaway husband, the child, the shame in her face. Her heavy, heavy face. Mah didn't hint, she threatened: "Death. I will jump from the Golden Gate. Take this child, this no-good child."

Tommie just happened to be locking up his factory. He remembered her. The pretty woman with the absent husband. Tommie consoled her. He offered her a job, but she didn't know anything about sewing, so Tommie taught her everything, from threading the machine to the secret seam that laid the interfacing flat, to how to lift the sewing foot and run a quick backstitch to secure the head of the zipper. At first, he teased that she had Sunday hands, but Mah quickly became his top seamstress.

The factory was sewing woolen coats. "Flipped," Tommie explained. "We work the summer fabrics in the winter, and the winter fabrics in the summer." All summer, the fans whirled, thick with dust.

From then on, whenever anyone mentioned Lyman Fu, Mah spat out three names: Gambler. Drunk. Corpse.

JUST before noon, Mah came home from Duckie's Mom's smelling like the perfume section of Woolworth's. Mason and I were still having coffee.

"Nice perm, Mrs. Leong," Mason said.

"Really? My face not too round?"

"No," Mason said. "You look like Miss Chinatown."

Mah laughed. "Bad boy! Talk pretty!" She put a pink box on the table. "Here, eat some dim sum."

AFTER Mason left, I helped Mah dress for Leon's welcome-home dinner. She'd made three new outfits but now she couldn't decide which one to wear: the gabardine pantsuit, the pink wool coat dress, or the A-line dress with the lace bib. She stood on the bed and looked at herself in the wide mirror of the dresser. She turned back and forth, pressing down on the pocket flaps, pulling at the pant seams. "My body's changed; nothing fits like before," she said.

"That looks okay," I said. I was sitting on the bed and could see myself in the mirror. "You know, Mason gave me a couple of driving lessons."

"Oh yeah?" she said. "It's always good to have a skill."

"Yesterday I parked on Broadway, you know, up near Taylor, the steep part," I said.

She frowned. "Does this look too tight?" She turned

sideways, sucked in; one hand pushed down on her belly.

I went over and tugged at the seams. "Maybe just a little," I said.

"You shouldn't sleep with him so much," she said.

I looked at her but didn't say anything.

She scrunched up her nose and scowled into the mirror. "My stomach sticks out too much. I'm going to try on the dress." She climbed off the bed.

"It's not that bad." I smoothed the footprints out of the bedspread.

"You never know. Mason's good now, but he could change," she said.

"He's not like that." My voice sounded harsh.

"Oh." Her mouth made that round O shape that meant she was embarrassed. "Tomorrow, I'm going to start exercising," she said. She peeled the waistband over her belly.

I stared at the top of her head. "You know Leon saw my father this trip," I said.

Her legs stopped moving from side to side and I saw the pink of her kneecaps. She looked up at me.

"What do you think of him, my father, now?"

"Waste of time," she muttered.

"Well," I said, looking away, "don't you ever think about him?"

"Why should I? That was so long ago." She took the dress off the hanger, bunched it up in her fist, and slipped it over her head.

I folded her pants. "Mah," I said, looking up, "I'm going to move to the Mission with Mason."

Her head slowly emerged from the folds of pink wool. She looked at me in the mirror. It was quiet for a long time. I thought, I do look like her. The shape of the face, the single fold above the eye, the smallish round mouth. I wonder, Will I be like her? Will I marry like her?

She turned around, away from me. The unzipped dress showed her back, still straight; her skin was still smooth. I went over to zip her up, and when she turned around, I said, "Wear this, you look great."

"No Chinese there, you know," she said.

"There are some," I said.

"Why not get married?" she asked. She still wouldn't look at me.

"I'll see how it goes," I said. For a minute I expected the worst, that she'd slap me, hit me with a hanger, call me names.

"Give it a test." She nodded, and then muttered, almost to herself, "Remember to have a way out."

THAT night, Ona and Nina wanted to go to a social event at Cameron House, so they couldn't make Leon's welcome-home dinner; I think they both knew I wanted to talk to Leon about my father.

At Tao-Tao's, Leon and Mah and Mason and I sat under my favorite Genthe photo of two little girls walking down an alley; they're holding hands, looking back. I had other favorites: the grocer with the beckoning smile, the shoe cobbler, the balloon peddler. We ordered enough food to invite the spirits of the oldtimers to join us. The food came steaming: clams and oysters and lobster and fresh sea bass, salt-and-pepper prawns and crab with black beans. Our hands were busy, messy from cracking the shells. I let Leon eat his first bowl of rice in peace.

When Mah handed him his second bowl, I refilled his

tea and asked him, "What did he look like? My father. You saw him, didn't you?"

Leon put an oyster in his mouth. "Dark," he said.

"Dark? Like how?" I asked.

"Like a coolie," Mason said.

Leon said in English, "Hey, you know that word?"

"Sure." Mason shrugged.

Leon grinned. "From the sun, like a dried plum."

"I thought he was some big developer," I said. "A man inside, behind a desk, you know?"

Mah muttered something as she cracked open a lobster claw.

"That's people talking," Leon said in Chinese.

I thought about it. "So, what'd you talk about?"

"Not much. I mentioned the situation here."

Whenever Leon used Chinese, he sounded more serious. So I waited for him to say more. "Well? What exactly did you say?"

"I told him about your Mah and me." Leon looked over at Mah, who was busy with a piece of crab.

"Well? What did he say?" I couldn't stand it; Leon was so slow sometimes it killed me. I wanted more. I gave my chopsticks three hard taps on the tabletop. Mah looked up, scowling.

"Easy." Mason put his hand on my leg. I sat back. He peeled a shrimp and put it on my plate, and I popped the whole thing into my mouth.

"What about me? Did he ask about me?"

"Sure," Leon said. "I told him that you'd finished school, stuff like that." He looked at Mah.

She gave him some fish. "Good piece," she said.

I wasn't satisfied. "How'd it end?"

"End?" He put the morsel in his mouth. "What else? Shook hands, said goodbye, long life, and good luck."

I listened to us eating—Mah and Leon, Mason and me—the soft suck of rice in our mouths, the click of the chopsticks against the bowls. These sounds were comfortable, and for a moment, I was tempted to fall back into the easiness of being Mah's daughter, of letting her be my whole life.

When Mah and Leon were first married, I was always surprised when he came home from his voyages. I expected him to change at sea; I think I even expected him to come back as my father. But it was always Leon Leong, in his starched whites, his burnt-sugar tan, his S.S. *Independent* laundry sack full of presents.

I finally saw what Mason had been saying all along: Mah loved Leon.

LEON once told me that what we hold in our heart is what matters.

The heart never travels.

I believe in holding still. I believe that the secrets we hold in our hearts are our anchors, that even the unspoken between us is a measure of our every promise to the living and to the dead. And all our promises, like all our hopes, move us through life with the power of an ocean liner pushing through the sea.

All my things fit into the back of Mason's cousin's Volvo. The last thing I saw as Mason backed out of the alley was the old blue sign, #2—4—6 UPDAIRE. No one has ever corrected it; someone repaints it every year. Like the oldtimer's photos, Leon's papers, and Grandpa

Leong's lost bones, it reminded me to look back, to remember.

I was reassured. I knew what I held in my heart would
guide me. So I wasn't worried when I turned that corner,
leaving the old blue sign, Salmon Alley, Mah and Leon—
everything—backdaire.